Dorothy Claes

A N D   T H E

Blood of the Tsar

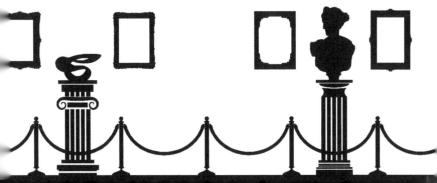

Dorothy Claes

AND THE

Blood of the Tsar

THE SILVER FOX MYSTERIES
BOOK THREE

C.P. MORGAN

Ordering Information:
www.authorcassandramorgan.com
www.amazon.com

First Printing: October 2019
White Whisker Publications

ISBN: 978-1-7330261-2-3

Special Thanks to

Aesteran Aaron, V. Meylakhov,
Lydia Sherrer, and Sasha De Vogel

A NOTE FROM THE AUTHOR

The Silver Fox Mysteries always carry a thread of truth in them, and I try to bring as much authenticity to my books as possible. But sometimes, authenticity may detract from a story. Because the reference to names in this book is not entirely accurate to Russia – characters might choose to refer to themselves or others differently in real-world situations – I want my readers to know it is entirely by choice on my part.

For the sake of keeping the characters straight for my readers, I have decided to use the First (Given) Name for my characters, unless it is combined with their Full Name. Tatiana does not become Tati or Tanya to her family, and then referred to by her formal first name for Dorothy, Sandi and the other non-family members.

As always, I hope the latest adventure of Dorothy and Solomon finds you well!

Happy Reading!

Love,
~ Cassie

ALEXEEV FAMILY TREE

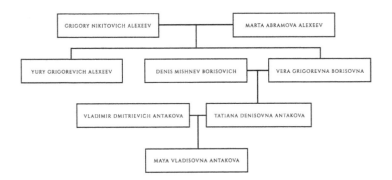

GRIGORY NIKITOVICH ALEXEEV — MARTA ABRAMOVA ALEXEEV

YURY GRIGOREVICH ALEXEEV

DENIS MISHNEV BORISOVICH

VERA GRIGOREVNA BORISOVNA

VLADIMIR DMITRIEVICH ANTAKOVA

TATIANA DENISOVNA ANTAKOVA

MAYA VLADISOVNA ANTAKOVA

ONE

A GENTLE SPRING BREEZE RUSTLED THE LEAVES of the yellow poplars that lined Waltham Street. The sun shone brightly, casting shadows on the sidewalk from the flower baskets that lightly bobbed back and forth on their little chains. Doors to the shops had been propped open, and the gentle notes of music carried down the street from one of the local restaurants.

With their sneakers slapping against the sidewalk in their haste, the school children skidded to a halt at the window to *Richard's Anecdotes*. They pressed their hands and faces against the glass, hoping to see the little black cat waiting for them as he did every day. Their cries of disappointment could be heard all the way to the street corner when the purple bed sat empty. They continued home, their shoes dragging and scraping against the pavement.

In the basement of the little antique shop, Solomon paced back and forth by the door that led to the spiral stone staircase. He could hear the children, and he pawed at the door, willing his human to open it for him. He needed to collect his daily pets, to assess each child's smell and assure they were well, but the woman didn't hear him.

Dorothy Claes stared at an artifact encased in glass upon a long wooden table that ran the length of the antique shop. She scribbled in a notebook and flipped through a stack of files from a dusty box on the table beside her. Solomon trotted up to her and jumped on the table. Beneath the glass case was an intricately embroidered piece of cloth. Horses and soldiers in medieval battle armor were stitched with such detail as to appear almost alive. He sniffed at the case, adding more nose prints to the glass.

Dorothy scribbled in her notebook again, ignoring the swish of Solomon's tail beside her. The Bayeux Tapestry was one of the oldest and most intact pieces of historical art she had come across in her time as a museum curator. It was also the only case she had found where Destin Hollanday and her father, Richard van Dame, had been on a Silver Fox mission together. After more scribbling, more tail flicks and annoyed paw licking from Solomon, Dorothy threw down her pen.

"This is useless," she mumbled, pulling a decorative hair stick from her bun and letting her silver tresses fall around her shoulders. A rather physical representation of her deflating hope. "I'll never find out what happened to Papa."

Solomon mewed softly, walking across the glass case to nuzzle Dorothy's hair. When he could sense her mood rise and tingle with happiness, he batted at the hair stick. It still contained traces of Red's scent, who was one of his favorite playmates.

"At least I still have you," Dorothy whispered, scratching the little cat behind his ear and petting him all the way to the tip of his kinked tail. The remnants of his fight with the *Jólakötturinn* would remain for the rest of his life, but they hadn't slowed him down. Clearly, as the hair stick fell to the floor and Solomon followed after it. Still, it was enough to give Dorothy pause, enough to make her consider Robbie Hodge's offer.

"Leave the Silver Foxes and I'll release your father's health records," he had said only a month ago. She hadn't seen nor heard from him since, though she always kept his card with her. Her hand brushed against its outline in her pocket instinctively as Solomon returned to the table, sans hair stick.

The antique phone by the door rang out, sending the little cat flailing, and the file Dorothy had been looking at cascading to the floor.

"Solomon!" she scolded, trying to gather as many papers as she could, the phone still clanging on its base across the room. She rose from the floor more slowly than she had a year ago and picked up the phone. "Hello?" she answered, breathless.

"Ms. Claes," said a friendly Irish accent.

"Dr. Jon. Are you here already?" Dorothy looked at the time on her cellphone. "It's only three—"

"I just landed at the airport," he said. "I want to make sure you're not going to cancel on me again."

Dorothy's shoulders sagged. She had avoided her last two physicals with Dr. Jon, but the pain in her knees was getting worse. Even if she was going to quit the Silver Foxes, the least she could do was get some proper medical care for her troubles before doing so.

"No, I'm not going to cancel."

"Good," said Dr. Jon. "Your father had the same aversion to me. I promise I don't bite. We took care of the vampire king back in the eighties anyhow."

Dorothy hesitated until Solomon winding around her ankles brought her to again. "I'm… glad to hear it?"

Dr. Jon laughed, and Dorothy relaxed. "I'll see you in a few hours. No accepting any cases until I've finished with you. Doctor's orders and that trumps Destin any day. See you soon, lass."

Dorothy set the phone back on its base and returned to the pile of papers strewn across the floor. She carefully tucked the Bayeux Tapestry case back into the folder, giving each paper one last look. She had scoured the file what felt like a thousand times, hoping to find some connection between Destin and her father, some reason he wouldn't tell her how Richard had really died. But nothing.

When the last of the papers had been gathered and reorganized, Dorothy pushed herself to her feet, knees cracking painfully, and the little black cat darting back and forth beneath her. A single scrap of paper came loose, and Dorothy watched it fall back to the floor. Solomon saw it too, his eyes dilating as it swept back and forth in the air until it was close enough to pounce on. He slammed it to the stone floor and bit the corner.

"Leave it," Dorothy said, shooing him away. She picked up the paper and studied it. "How..." she whispered, opening the file in her hand. She had been through the dratted thing so many times, and yet she'd missed this.

The contents of the note made no sense. It was scribbled haphazardly, strange symbols interspersed with various language alphabets. She shoved the scrap of paper in her pocket and headed out of the artifact vault. Solomon bounded ahead of her, mewing with each stone step, and his kinked tail swishing with each disgruntled huff. They emerged into Dorothy's apartment, and she pushed the bookcase closed behind her before righting the book on the shelf that acted as the latch.

She heard Solomon pad down the apartment stairs toward the antique shop. He jiggled the French handle of the door in his front paws and pushed it open, running straight for the front window and his little purple bed. Dorothy shook her head, stepping into the shop after him and closing the avocado-green door.

"Afternoon, ma'am," said Aaron from behind the counter.

"Hello, Aaron," Dorothy greeted her assistant. She scanned the contents of the shop, not taking in a single thing. She fidgeted with her blouse and paced between the rows of antiques.

"Everything all right, ma'am?"

"Hmm?"

Aaron set down the inventory book he'd been writing in and came to the front of the counter. He set his hands on Dorothy's shoulders, steadying her nervous twitches.

"What?" she asked.

"Relax," Aaron said, his light Jamaican accent soothing her nerves. "Dr. Jon used to take care of

Richard. He'll take care of you."

Dorothy smiled, and she felt some of her tension melt away. "Thank you, Aaron. I'm fine. It's just—"

"If he doesn't, he'll have me to answer to." Aaron winked at her, then returned to his book behind the counter.

The next few hours passed slower than Mary Pat driving to the family reunion each year. Dorothy checked the time on her phone every few minutes, flitting back and forth from one email account to another. She checked the auction sites until she had clicked on the same fake Ming Dynasty vase four times. Finally, she found a polishing rag in the back room and set to work on an array of silver utensils that had been sitting on the same bureau for the last three years.

The bell above the door chimed for the second time that day, and Dorothy watched Solomon leave his bed to greet their guest. The man smiled, adjusting a large backpack over his shoulder and setting his briefcase on the floor. He was a short, husky man with a dark amber complexion, his hair flecked in salt and pepper.

"Well, hello, Solomon," said Dr. Jon, reaching down to scoop the cat into his arms. "How's that tail of yours?"

Solomon pushed into Dr. Jon's chin. He wiggled in his arms until he hit the man in the face with his tail

7

and jumped down.

"Hello, Dr. Jon. I don't know if you remember me," said Aaron.

Dr. Jon stepped over the cat who insisted on staying plastered to his ankles and approached the counter. "Aye, it's Aaron, right?"

Aaron flashed a smile and nodded.

"You worked for Richard, didn't you?"

"Yes, sir," said Aaron, standing a little straighter. "Now I work for Ms. Claes."

"I'll be out of a job soon if he keeps it up," said Dorothy, joining the two men and holding her hand out to the doctor.

"Glad to see you didn't scurry off before I got here," Dr. Jon said, shaking Dorothy's hand. "Do you have someone to take care of you for the next few days?"

"No, but I'll—" Dorothy watched concern rise in Aaron's face. "I'll be fine. It's the weekend," she finished. "Besides, Mary Pat would probably cause more harm than good."

Dr. Jon hesitated, casting a sidelong glance at Aaron.

"I'll do it," Aaron chimed. "Whatever you need, I'll help."

"No, it's fine, Aaron—"

"It's a good idea to stay off your feet as much as possible for the next few days."

"They're just cortisone shots, Dr. Jon. I'm not having surgery."

Dr. Jon turned to Aaron. "She needs to ice every few hours and standing too long to cook is out of the question."

Aaron nodded, avoiding Dorothy's exasperated look. "I can handle it, sir," he said.

"Good. Now, let's get started, shall we?" Dr. Jon gestured toward the door to the apartments as Aaron returned to the counter, pulling his phone out and looking up what Dorothy only assumed were dinner recipes on the internet.

She sighed and held the door open, first for Solomon, and then Dr. Jon. The man nodded when he reached the landing at the top of the stairs. Richard's old desk still sat to one side, covered with slightly neater stacks of paper, bills, and the odd cup of cold tea. He set his briefcase and medical bag beside the desk, continuing to take in the changes Dorothy had made.

"This should do just fine," he said. He opened the bag and pulled out a set of blue medical scrubs. He handed them to Dorothy and began emptying the remaining contents of the bag onto the desk corner.

Dorothy looked at the scrubs in her hands, and her heart began to race. The day of Frank's surgery came unwanted into her mind's eye. The doctors had worn

9

the same blue scrubs, though theirs had been covered in blood—Frank's blood. The surgery had been successful, but there had been a risk. There had always been a risk. Somehow, even though she was sure she was misremembering, another memory flashed into her mind. She could see the nurses at the hospital huddled over her father's body, checking machines, drawing blood, and all wearing the same blue scrubs.

Solomon seemed to appear out of nowhere. He gave one of his concerned little trills and rubbed against her legs. Dorothy exhaled, not realizing she had been holding her breath.

"Dorothy?" Dr. Jon asked.

Dorothy looked up, seeing something other than the pale blue scrubs for the first time. "I'm fine. Everything is fine," she said.

"There's nothing to be scared over." A gentle smile spread across Dr. Jon's face.

Dorothy nodded. "I know. I'm not. I—I haven't been to a doctor in years. It—It never seems to bode well for my family." She looked at the scrubs still clutched in her hands. "You had to know something about my father's health."

Dr. Jon straightened and sighed. "Dorothy, you know I can't."

"You say you *can't*, but not that you *won't*." Her eyes

held his gaze, firm and unyielding.

Dr. Jon was silent for several moments. He opened and closed his mouth as he gathered his thoughts. "The last time I saw your father, which was a few months before his death, he was perfectly healthy. He had a few minor kidney stones, but nothing life-threatening. And arthritis in his hands and knees, which we were treating with cortisone injections."

"And after he died?" Dorothy pressed. "The coroner's report is sealed away with his file."

Dr. Jon bit his lip and shook his head. "Look, Dorothy, I joined the Foxes because I wanted to make a difference beyond my work at the hospital. I knew there was more for me out there than being stuck in a surgery room or in a lab. If I betray the Foxes, it's all over for me."

"What do you mean? I'm sure you'll find another residency or retire or—"

Dr. Jon shook his head. "I've already said more than I should. When you've changed, I'll run you through some breathing exercises to get your blood pressure down. It's as high as a young man at a stag party."

Dorothy looked down at the little cat who had remained by her feet, pawing at her legs. He gazed up at her with his bright green eyes, and not for the first time, she wished she knew what he was trying to say.

"I'm on your side, Dorothy," stated Dr. Jon. "I really am."

Dorothy turned, heading for the bathroom. "I'm not entirely sure what side that is, Dr. Jon."

TWO

THE BREATHING EXERCISES HELPED TO BRING Dorothy's blood pressure within a normal range for the official record. They didn't help, however, with the injections. Dr. Jon's hands were steady, but the procedure took longer than she had anticipated. Though Solomon standing on the doctor's back as he bent over her knee probably didn't help, either. When he finished, Dorothy exhaled, then immediately cried out when he set an ice pack on her knee.

"A little warning next time," she huffed, grabbing the pack before it slid down her leg.

"I'm putting an ice pack on your knee now," said Dr. Jon with a cheeky grin.

Solomon mewed and rubbed against the man's side. Dorothy glared.

Dr. Jon chuckled, giving the little cat a scratch. "I'm

THE SILVER FOX MYSTERIES

not kidding about keeping that ice on, lass."

"Yes, doctor," Dorothy said, readjusting her seat and wincing.

There was a soft knock on the apartment door. They heard the latch and Aaron's voice. "Dr. Jon? Ms. Claes?"

"What are you still doing here?" Dorothy called.

She heard his footsteps on the carpeted stairs and the rustling of a plastic bag. "I hope Chinese is all right," Aaron said, holding up two plastic delivery bags.

"Oh, Aaron, you didn't—"

Aaron set the bags on the counter in the little kitchenette, pulling out his phone as he approached Dorothy. "I knew you'd say that," he said and handed her the phone.

Her scowl of confusion deepened as she took the phone and watched as Dr. Jon spoke quietly to Aaron.

"Hello?" Dorothy said, keeping one eye on the pair in front of her.

"How's my foxy lady?" asked a familiar voice.

"Red?" Dorothy cried, lurching forward as the voice of her beau greeted her. The ice pack slid forward, landing with a thud on her foot.

"Now take it easy," Red said. "Aaron had good reason to call."

"Red, I'm perfectly fine. It's just a couple of knee

injections," Dorothy scoffed. "Which, I might add, you may or may not have had a hand in worsening said condition over Valentine's Day." Solomon jumped into her lap and began pawing at the phone. She screamed in pain when he stepped on her knee, and he bolted to the floor, his fur standing on end.

Aaron and Dr. Jon looked up from their conversation, following Dorothy's gaze to the fluffy cat standing between them.

She heard Red on the phone she now held at arm's length. "Dorothy? Dorothy!"

She slowly brought the phone back to her ear. "It was just Solomon stepping on me. I may not be a young girl anymore, but I'm not an invalid," she mumbled to Red.

Aaron walked toward her and lifted the ice pack from the floor, gently handing it to her before rejoining the doctor.

"Dorothy, no one is trying to say you're incapable, but you have people there who care about you. Let them take care of you."

Dorothy sighed. She opened her mouth to protest, but Red was faster.

"You're still a strong, independent woman. Don't worry."

Dorothy rolled her eyes. "Red, I'm not that terrible.

I've just been on my own for so long."

"Well, you aren't anymore. You're the closest thing that young man has to family in the States. Let him do something for you for a change. And I'm only a phone call away if you ever need to vent about Solomon or berate me for Valentine's Day."

This time, Dorothy laughed. "Well, it wasn't *all* bad."

"That's the foxy lady I know. Now, give the phone back to Aaron so I can tell him not to nag you too much."

Dorothy smirked and called Aaron back. He ducked into the kitchenette with the phone as Dr. Jon dodged past him.

"Sounds like you're all set then, *mo chara*," Dr. Jon said.

"Sounds like it."

"Aaron promised he'll bring you something homemade tomorrow." Dr. Jon winked, and Dorothy shook her head.

The man looked over his shoulder at Aaron, who was still speaking to Red. "You'll figure it out, Dorothy. Don't worry yourself. And when you do, I'll be here."

He reached out a hand to her. She took it, feeling a tiny scrap of paper. Eyes narrowed, she shook his hand, carefully sliding the paper between her fingers.

Dr. Jon shook Aaron's hand, and the young man

followed him down the apartment steps so he could lock the shop door behind him. Dorothy quickly tucked the paper out of sight and waited for Aaron to return.

"So, what are we having for dinner?" she asked when he reappeared, dodging Solomon as he stepped into the kitchenette.

Aaron beamed. "I wasn't sure what you liked, so I got a few different things," he said and began digging through the bags. "We have fried dumplings and egg rolls. I got plenty of rice here. There's lemon chicken and moo goo gai pan…"

Under Dorothy's careful direction, Aaron found plates, cups and silverware. He fed Solomon his dinner and even cleaned the dishes after they had eaten. Dorothy watched him work from the comfort of her father's old armchair. Frank used to do the washing up after dinner as well, and Solomon wound around Aaron's ankles as he used to do with Frank. She wondered for a moment what it would have been like if she and Frank had been blessed with children. She smiled at the thought, thinking of a little Aaron tearing into a stack of birthday presents or running along the banks of the Scottish shore.

"I'll be back in the morning," said Aaron, bringing Dorothy out of her thoughts.

"If you bring me anything, I better get the receipts," she asserted, eyeing Aaron from across the room.

"Yes, ma'am." Aaron gave Solomon a last pet and headed down the stairs.

Dorothy waited until she heard the bell above the shop door. She reached into the pocket of the scrubs she still wore and pulled out the paper Dr. Jon had given her. She had expected an address, perhaps a phone number, some kind of clue that brought her closer to the truth about her father. Instead, she saw two words scribbled in haste: *Materia Prima*.

Solomon padded back up the stairs and leapt onto the chair arm. He sat and licked his paw, his ears pricked forward as if waiting for Dorothy to acknowledge him. Dorothy stared at the paper for several long moments. Studying the height of the letters, she hoped the words were an anagram to something else. She flipped it over and over, but there were no additional messages or clues. There was nothing.

She reached forward and removed the ice pack from her knee. The area had already begun to swell, just as Dr. Jon had said it might. Solomon pressed his cold nose against her arm. She scratched his ears, gathering her strength before pushing herself out of the chair and hobbling to the bedroom. These were going to be the longest two days of her life.

Aaron arrived bright and early the next morning as promised. She could hear him in the kitchenette, trying to be quiet, but to no avail. Solomon yawned and stretched at her feet. She sat up reaching for his paws. He grabbed her finger in his toes and nuzzled her hand. He had spent most of the night pressed into her leg, and the heat against her knee had been a welcome relief from the ice packs. She stood, bracing herself for the pain, but only slight discomfort radiated from the injection sites. The moment her feet hit the floor, Solomon bounded from the bed and began meowing for his breakfast.

"In a minute," she scolded, though it never phased the little cat. He always acted as if his last meal were three years ago. She showered as quickly as her knee would allow and dressed before heading into the main apartment.

The smell of burnt toast and sausage met her as she rounded the corner into the sitting room. Aaron looked up from his cooking, his apron streaked with butter. He tried to force a smile but immediately turned back to the smoking bread in the griddle pan.

"Good morning," Dorothy said, taking the spatula

from his hand. "What are we having?"

"Uh, well, I was trying to—"

"Here. You've got your heat too high. Like this." Dorothy adjusted the knobs on the stove and showed him where the cooking spray was.

"I've got it, ma'am," Aaron insisted, ushering her back to the armchair with a fresh ice pack. He set another piece of French toast on the pan and opened a can of food for Solomon, who had been loudly protesting at his feet since they'd left the bedroom.

Aaron flipped the piece of bread and handed Dorothy a steaming mug of tea, which she accepted graciously. She blew across the surface, watching Aaron over the top of her cup. Breakfast had been Frank's specialty, and Red seemed to have a knack for it as well. Aaron learned quickly, and though the edges of the bread were slightly blackened and the eggs a bit overdone, Dorothy admitted it was a relief not to cook.

They sat across from each other, Dorothy in her father's armchair and Aaron cross-legged on the sofa. Solomon flitted back and forth between them, pawing at their legs and begging for treats. She didn't say anything, but she saw Aaron slip Solomon a piece of sausage when he thought she wasn't looking.

"How are you and Lauren?" Dorothy asked, making conversation as she polished off the last of her eggs.

Aaron swallowed his bite of sausage and shrugged. "I'm not sure. She said she wants to take a break. I think she was upset I didn't want to move to Cancun with her."

"Cancun? That's awfully far."

Aaron shrugged again. "It's closer to Jamaica, but I like it here."

Dorothy clicked her tongue and sighed. "I'm sorry, Aaron."

The young man sat straighter and forced a smile. "I've got family here too," he said. "Oh! I almost forgot!" He unfolded himself from the couch and hurried down the apartment steps, his breakfast plate still in hand and Solomon trailing after him.

Dorothy chuckled. She pushed herself to her feet and slowly made her way toward the kitchenette. She leaned against the counter and heard Aaron and Solomon make their way back up the stairs. Aaron set his plate on the counter, and Solomon immediately jumped up, helping himself to the remaining syrup and burnt toast edges left behind.

The young man beamed at Dorothy and held out an old, antique cane to her. "I found this in the back room a few days ago. I was going to ask you about it, but I think you could use it more than a display case right now."

With an expert touch, Dorothy accepted the cane, running her hand over the design of the crook, topped with a polished silver detail.

"I knew you wouldn't want to be stuck up here all day," Aaron mumbled and rubbed the back of his neck shyly.

Dorothy pulled away from the counter, leaning into the cane and testing it. She smiled, reaching for his hand. "Thank you, Aaron," she said, squeezing his fingers. Aaron squeezed her hand back and picked up the plate from the counter. "I'll finish cleaning up here if you want to go open the shop," she said, taking the plate from him.

Aaron nodded and headed toward the apartment door, Solomon in tow with syrup on the tips of his ears.

Saturdays were typically busy for *Richard's Anecdotes*, and today was no exception. Dorothy was thankful for Aaron's gift, and though she hated to admit it, for Aaron's constant nagging at her to sit still. After his third reprimand, he wheeled the office chair from the back room and demanded she sit for at least an hour. Dorothy obliged, though she had to be careful not to catch Solomon's paws or tail.

By the end of the day, most of the swelling that had accumulated throughout the night had subsided, and she could walk almost completely unassisted. She returned the chair to the back room as Aaron flipped the sign on the door to *Closed* and locked the dead bolt.

"I'll be up soon to start dinner," he called as he locked one of the glass cases. "I just have to finish entering in the last couple items from the auction sale today."

"Of course, Mr. Williams," Dorothy said slyly. She reached for the handle of the avocado-green door and hesitated.

"Aaron," she said. Aaron paused over the keyboard. "Do you know anything about something called the *Materia Prima*?"

Aaron's brow furrowed. "*Materia Prima*? Well, it's Latin, of course. The Materia Primal? The Prime Material? Why? What's up?"

Dorothy shook her head. "It's nothing. Just a silly question." She turned toward the stairs, waving her hand dismissively. "Forget I said anything."

"Is it about that scroll?"

Dorothy turned back, her knee beginning to throb again. "Scroll?"

"The one Richard was looking into. Did you find something new?"

Dorothy stared at Aaron, unsure what to say. She had all but given up on deciphering that scroll and had tucked it away in her father's vault. Her mind raced, and she thought of the strange scrap of paper that had fallen out of the Bayeux Tapestry file the day before. The symbols had been similar.

"Ms. Claes?"

Dorothy blinked. "Yes, well, no. Perhaps. I'm not sure."

"Do you want me to look into it for you?"

"No, that's not necessary."

Aaron nodded, though he seemed to sulk as Dorothy turned back toward the apartment stairs. Going down had been easier than going up. By the time she reached the top, her knee was throbbing even more. She pulled an ice pack from the freezer and eyed the bookcase, sitting in the armchair with a huff.

Solomon rubbed against her legs, and she used the end of her cane to play with him as the ice slowly penetrated her knee. She almost didn't notice her phone buzzing on the end table beside her. She fumbled for it, accidentally whacking Solomon between the ears with the cane as she swiped to answer the call, her thumb hitting the speaker phone button in her haste.

"Oh, little buddy!" she cried. "I'm so sorry! Hello?"

"I'm not sure who you're calling 'Little Buddy,' but I'm perfectly well, thank you very much," came Destin's smooth voice.

"Hello, Destin. You know Dr. Jon has me on orders

not to take any missions for a couple days."

"Yes, I'm well aware. This one isn't urgent, and I am more in need of the *other* agent at your address than you. No offense, Fennec."

"Solomon?" Dorothy said, and the little cat trilled at the sound of his name.

"Yes, Solomon. If I'm correct, the Constellation Faberge egg can only be obtained by the true Romanov heir. Alexei's blood was easy enough to come by, but the cat was the more difficult aspect—until recently anyhow. We know Solomon can handle himself in the high-stress situations of our missions."

"Slow down, Destin. I don't under—"

"You don't need to understand. I just wanted you to know that Artie is flying Sandi out to you tomorrow. He'll brief you on your mission. Your knee should be well enough to travel in a few days. Per Dr. Jon, anyway."

Dorothy rolled her eyes. "Thanks for the warning," she said.

"You're welcome. Heal up, Fennec. Russia waits for no one."

The phone went silent, and Dorothy returned it to the end table beside her. When she looked up, she saw Aaron standing transfixed at the top of the stairs.

THREE

SOLOMON FLICKED HIS TAIL IN DOROTHY'S FACE, leaping off her lap to greet Aaron. The young man scooped the cat into his arms and cleared his throat. "I—uh—I finished that inventory."

"Oh, good." Dorothy nudged the phone on the end table, trying to act casual. "I have a guest coming in tomorrow."

"Mr. Sandi," Aaron stated.

"Uh, yes." Dorothy had forgotten Aaron's familiarity with the other agents through her father. She licked her lips and stood. "I'm going to get some linens out. The kitchen's all yours." She smiled and leaned against her cane.

"Any particular requests?"

Solomon meowed loudly and rubbed Aaron's chin.

"Whatever you're in the mood for, Chef Williams,"

she said and headed toward the bathroom. She heard Solomon bring Aaron his jingle ball and hoped his antics would be a distraction for the strange conversation he had just overheard.

Opening the linen closet, she stared at the contents inside. How much had Aaron heard? Was he now in danger? Dr. Jon's words echoed in her mind. *If I betray the Foxes, it's all over for me.* What lengths would Destin go to keep the Foxes a secret? She wanted to tell Aaron. It certainly would make her travels easier to explain, and his help with research could be more specific.

She swallowed. No. She wouldn't risk it. She wiped a stray tear from her cheek, and it surprised her. The thought of losing Aaron, the thought of anything happening to him…

There was a crash in the kitchen and Solomon zoomed past the bathroom door, his tail floofed to its fullest extent. Dorothy gathered sheets, a blanket and a spare pillow into her arms and ventured back into the apartment.

She found Solomon inching closer to Aaron, who was on his knees cleaning up tomato sauce that had splattered all over the floor. She set her load on the couch and put a hand on her hip, the other still leaning into the cane. Aaron looked slowly up at her, his face flushing.

"Looks like it's pizza tonight," Dorothy announced.

Aaron's face fell, and he returned to the mess before him, barely flicking Solomon's ball when the little cat brought it to him.

"Oh, Aaron!" said Dorothy. "It's all right! You don't even have to do this. Any of this."

"But I want to," Aaron insisted, his voice small. "You've done so much for me, and—"

Dorothy hobbled through the living room and into the kitchen. Aaron looked up at her, his dark eyes glassy with tears.

"Aaron, family doesn't recognize tit for tat. Not in this house, anyway." She reached into the cupboard above the fridge and pulled out several rolls of paper towels. "Believe me, I would rather have tomato sauce on my floor any day than ask Mary Pat to help me."

A smile flicked across Aaron's face, then catching himself, he bit his lip. He caught Dorothy's eye, and she winked at him. He let out a chuckle, relaxing and accepted one of the paper towel rolls.

"That's better," she said. "What do you like on your pizza?"

"Anything except jalapenos and anchovies," he said.

Dorothy raised an eyebrow at him. "Even pineapple?"

Aaron laughed. "Especially pineapple when it's on

barbeque chicken pizza." His eyes caught sight of the phone still sitting on the end table, and he cleared his throat. "I'll finish cleaning this up," he said, quickly returning to the tomato mess Solomon had begun helping himself to.

The pizza was greasy and delicious, but Dorothy sensed a tension in the air that hadn't been there before. She told herself she was reading into things, that the prescription painkillers Dr. Jon had given her were too strong and were making her paranoid. But Aaron had most definitely heard her conversation with Destin. How much he could have gleaned, she had no idea. She hoped it wasn't enough to send him down a rabbit hole of research that ended in him mysteriously disappearing, and Destin once again unable to provide any answers.

The thought sent a physical chill down her spine. She shook it off and offered a piece of pineapple to Solomon.

"All right, ma'am?" Aaron asked when he saw her shake.

"Just a chill," Dorothy said. "Probably too much time with the ice pack."

"Here." Aaron stood and held out his hand for the pack. Dorothy handed it to him, then set her empty plate on the floor for Solomon to lick clean.

"There's a new bagel shop that opened a few blocks from my apartment," Aaron said from the kitchen. "I still have a coupon for a free dozen. That should be plenty for us and Mr. Sandi."

Dorothy hesitated, and the smile on Aaron's face began to disappear.

"You have done more than I could ever ask for," Dorothy said. "I'm doing much better now, and with Sandi coming, I'm sure he can help."

"Oh," said Aaron. "Okay."

Dorothy bit her tongue, Dr. Jon's words still ringing in her mind. It was for his own safety, she told herself.

"Take some pizza home with you and promise me you'll spend the day having fun."

Aaron consented, then turned to the sink to begin the washing up.

Despite the warm spring air and the lack of an ice pack on her knee that night, Dorothy felt cold. She huddled under the blankets, Solomon tucked up next to her. He sprawled on his back, paws twitching in the air as he snuggled into her. Outside, the world was quiet, but Dorothy's mind hummed. The ancient scroll her father had been studying. The Bayeux Tapestry. *Materia Prima*. What did it all mean? The stone steps down to her father's vault were still too steep and precarious for her to risk just yet. The last thing she needed was for Sandi to find her at the bottom of the winding stone stair in the morning, because whose side was Sandi on? Were there sides at all? Caprice would side with Destin, Dorothy was sure of it. She knew she'd have done the same for Frank, or even Red. Dr. Jon knew something, but it was hard to say where he toed the line. And what line was that exactly? Dorothy still had no idea.

Solomon snored quietly beside her as the sky outside her window began to turn a dark gray against the black of night. She hadn't slept at all. She rolled over, shoving the little cat out of the way. 4:45 She could still get a few hours of sleep. If she closed her eyes right now. If she shut off her mind for just a moment. Let the fears and mystery subside for just—

The sound of Dorothy's cell phone cut through the quiet of the morning air, sending Solomon bolting off the bed. Her eyes shot open, and she scrambled to reach for the nightstand and the brightly glowing object that screamed to be answered.

"Hello?" she croaked, her voice hoarse.

"Fennec *nǚ shì*?" said a man's voice on the other end.

"Sandi?" Dorothy asked as she rubbed the sleep from her eyes. "Are you here already?"

"I am in car from airport. I be there in two hours," he said through a heavy Mandarin accent.

"Great. Thank you. I'll see you when you get here."

"*Yī huǐ er jiàn,*" he said, hanging up the phone.

Solomon returned to the bed, snuggling back against her. Dorothy rubbed her face and felt the bags under her eyes. She set an alarm for an hour, and this time, drifted to sleep as soon as the little cat crawled into her arms and tucked his head beneath her chin.

The hour went quickly, as Dorothy had expected, though neither she nor Solomon were ready to get up. She left him burrowed under the blanket while she showered and started a pot of water to heat on the stove. She popped a few slices of toast in the toaster, and Solomon came bounding from the bedroom for his own breakfast. He wound around her ankles, rubbing on her cane and meowing, though his dramatics were as if he hadn't been fed for a whole ten years this time.

Dorothy rolled her eyes but obliged the little cat with a tin of food. His bent tail flicked back and forth happily as he ate his breakfast in under five minutes. She counted the number of cat food cans she still had in the cupboard. She didn't know how long she'd be gone, but she hoped it was enough to get her through the mission.

Solomon polished off his food and sauntered into the living room to clean his face. Dorothy glanced at the microwave clock. Sandi would arrive any moment. Leaving the little cat on the arm of the chair to scrub his face and ears, she headed down the apartment steps. With each step, she thanked Aaron for finding the cane. Most of the intense pain had subsided, but a dull ache still persisted, mostly at the injection site, and she hoped it too would fade. Preferably sooner than later.

She flicked on the lights to the shop just as a figure stepped onto the front stoop. Dorothy walked closer, peering through the slats in the door blinds. It was a tiny man with thinning white hair, dressed in a button-down shirt and slacks. He saw Dorothy through the window and bowed.

Dorothy unlocked the door smiling as she held it wide. "Mr. Sandi," she greeted him.

The man bowed again, then entered. He set a small suitcase at his feet, taking in the little shop. "You did not change it," he said.

Dorothy followed his gaze. "No, I suppose I haven't." Her father's layout had been efficient, and there had been little need to rearrange. But even some of the larger pieces that had been there before her father's death were exactly where they had always been. It gave Dorothy pause. Could there be more hidden secrets in the shop she had yet to discover?

The tea kettle whistled on the stove upstairs, and Sandi smiled when he heard it. "I hear you drink tea," he said. "I bring some."

"I can't wait to try it," said Dorothy, ushering him toward the avocado-green door.

Sandi picked up his suitcase and headed up the apartment stairs. The wrinkles on his face said he was old enough to be her father, but the spring in his step said otherwise. Dorothy struggled to keep pace, and her knee throbbed when she finally reached the top. Solomon had already taken the liberty to introduce himself and was accepting ear scratches from Sandi.

"This is the other agent?" Sandi chuckled. He frowned when he turned to Dorothy and saw her wince as she climbed the last step. "You hurt."

"I'm fine." Dorothy waved off his concern.

Sandi squinted at her, likely unbelieving, but did not reply.

"Please, make yourself comfortable," said Dorothy, gesturing toward the living room.

Sandi returned the smile and set his suitcase on the couch beside the linens Dorothy had laid out. He opened it and pulled out a small bag of loose leaf tea amongst the tightly rolled clothes in neat little rows. He smelled the bag and turned to Dorothy smiling.

"Here," he said, "I'll make it." He bowed and waited for her to step aside. With air of familiarity, he threw open the cupboard filled with food items and turned with smirk. "This you change," he said.

With a little help, Sandi found the teacups and tea strainers. He carefully measured out the tea leaves and stood over the cups as they steeped, checking his watch every few minutes. Dorothy had never seen Solomon so quiet and curious. Occasionally, Sandi would look down at the little cat and say something in Mandarin to him. Solomon would tilt his head to the other side, his ears turning and listening. When he was finally happy with his concoction, Sandi picked up the teacups and brought them to the sitting room, gliding across the floor with a grace Dorothy expected from the likes of Miss Kitty. He handed her the tea and took a seat on the couch.

"Thank you," Dorothy said.

"*Bié jiàn wài,*" Sandi replied.

Dorothy blew across the top of her cup. The tea smelled divine. Spicy like ginger with a hint of floral notes. Sandi set his cup on the end table and reached for his suitcase. He pulled out a small, black box, handing it to Dorothy with a small bow of his head.

"Oh, thank you," Dorothy said again, now beginning to feel a bit strange with all the gifts Sandi was bestowing upon her.

Sandi nodded at her, encouraging her to open it. Dorothy set her cup down just as Solomon bounded into her lap. She gasped in pain when his paw landed on her knee. A few days to recover indeed.

"Here," said Sandi, "You hurt. Let me." He stood from the couch and knelt on the floor beside Dorothy.

"No, really, I'm okay."

Sandi raised an eyebrow at her. He pulled an identical black box from his pocket and opened it. Inside was a small brass ear cuff. He took it from the box and placed it on his ear. Then he nodded toward Dorothy's black box. Perplexed and still slightly in pain, Dorothy opened her box. Inside was another brass ear cuff. She clipped it on, and the world took on a muffled whooshing noise.

"There, better?" Sandi asked.

Dorothy sat back. She could hear Sandi's distant Mandarin as though carried on the wind of the strange ear cuff, but the words came to her ear as clear as any English.

"Is this an artifact?" she questioned, unable to hide the awe in her voice.

"It is," Sandi confirmed. "Taken from the city of Babel. It allows us to communicate even speaking two different languages."

Dorothy glanced at Solomon, who stood on the arm of the chair beside her, and Sandi followed her gaze.

"I'm afraid it does not cross species."

Dorothy felt how far her mouth had fallen open. She

closed it and chuckled.

"Can I help you with your pain?" Sandi asked.

"I'll be okay," Dorothy assured him. "I just haven't taken my medicine yet this morning."

"If I might try some *chi* energy," Sandi offered, rubbing his hands together.

"*Chi*?" Dorothy asked, unable to hide the skepticism in her voice. Could the Babel translator also translate inflection?

"It's not magic, *nǚ shì*," Sandi said with an understanding smile. "And in truth, magic is simply science that most do not yet understand. This is how the artifacts work, yes?"

Dorothy opened her mouth to speak as Solomon pawed at her arm, mewing pitifully. Sandi was right. "Oh, all right," she said, more to Solomon than to Sandi.

The man smiled and knelt at Dorothy's feet, continuing to rub his hands together, his eyes closed in concentration. He moved his hands back and forth in a deliberate and practiced dance. The little cat watched with fascination. After a moment, Sandi opened his eyes and offered his hands to Solomon. The cat sniffed and rubbed on his fingers in approval. With a smile, Sandi set his hands on Dorothy's knee.

The heat was more than Dorothy expected, but

37

the pulsating energy she felt surprised her more. She sat still, afraid moving might disrupt Sandi's concentration, or worse, cause her injury. Solomon sat beside her, his pupils dilated, fixated on Sandi's hands. When he finished, Sandi pulled his hands away and bowed to Dorothy. The heat slowly dissipated, as did her pain. Dorothy rubbed her knee, and Solomon stepped into her lap to sniff it.

"Do you feel better?" Sandi asked, moving back to the couch.

"Yes," Dorothy said, surprised. "Thank you."

"It is nothing. Now, we should discuss our mission." Sandi reached into his pocket and pulled out a tiny microchip. "Do you have your Fox tablet?"

Dorothy stood from the chair, not thinking to grab her cane until she was halfway to her bedroom, where the device lay charging. She hurried back to the sitting room with a renewed vigor and handed the tablet to Sandi. He accepted the device, immediately flipping it over and popping off the back panel. His agent profile said he worked as a computer programmer writing code. It also listed *Hacking* as a skill, though Dorothy knew little of what that meant. He placed the chip with delicate fingers, then replaced the panel and hit the power button.

A silver fox flashed across the screen before a grainy

video of Destin loaded and began playing.

"Hello, foxes. I much prefer Artie brief you on your cases, but he will not be transporting you this time."

Dorothy and Sandi looked at each other in surprise. Solomon settled on the couch beside Sandi as Destin's video played. "This case is rather sensitive, which is why I am keeping its information limited to you. Furthermore, the Foxes currently do not have any alliances within the bounds of Russia. Which means once you're in there, you're on your own."

"On our own?" Dorothy asked.

Sandi shrugged. "I've never had such a thing happen before."

"As I said," Destin's voice continued, "this case is sensitive. At the beginning of the twentieth century, Russia was experiencing a revolution, or rather, a revolt, against Nicholas II. The Tsar knew this and began making plans. For years he had been working with the famous craftsman Peter Carl Faberge to create Easter gifts for his family. In 1916, he commissioned Faberge to create a very special egg, one that would ensure the rightful heir could reclaim the throne of Russia."

The screen split, and Destin tapped some buttons on his keyboard, bringing up an image of a brilliant blue Faberge egg.

"Grigory Nikitovich Alexeev was a Russian military

officer whose family's connection to the royal Tsar dates back centuries. When the Constellation Egg was completed, it was given to his ancestors for safekeeping. Nicholas believed that his son and heir, Alexei Nikolaevich Romanov, would one day reclaim the throne of Russia."

Destin pushed more buttons, and a new image appeared on the screen, this one, taken from an old photograph, showed a young boy and his cat.

"But it wasn't enough that Alexei have the egg in his possession, and Nicholas was no fool, knowing it might not even be Alexei, but one of his descendants. Alexei was afflicted with hemophilia, a condition passed through the line of Queen Victoria on his mother's side. Whoever would take control of the Constellation Egg's power would have to prove themselves a descendant by blood."

Reaching into a drawer off camera, Destin produced a tiny vial. Dorothy squinted at the grainy image, though she was confident she knew what it contained.

"Alexei's blood was easy enough to come by, and I have concealed it inside a decoy inhaler canister to help get it through Russian customs undetected."

Sandi reached into his suitcase and withdrew a large padded envelope. Among the papers was the inhaler. He held it out to Solomon to inspect, then handed it to Dorothy.

"There is one last requirement for getting the egg," said Destin, putting the vial of blood back into his desk drawer. "Alexei was known to be a great cat lover. So much so that even though he suffered severely from hemophilia, he would not give up his beloved cat Kot'ka. For this reason, Nicholas told Faberge to make sure the rightful heir to the Russian throne was also a cat lover. I have little intelligence on how this might work. It may be all that is needed are a few strands of cat hair. Or it could be a descendant of Kot'ka is required. I do not know. Which is why I need you to be extra careful."

The image of Alexei and Kot'ka disappeared, and Destin's figure took up the full screen again.

"The Constellation Egg is called such for a reason. The alignment of the stars on the egg will soon match those above the Winter Palace. I do not know what will happen when that alignment occurs, but I cannot risk the egg falling into the wrong hands.

"Grigory Nikitovich Alexeev, the guardian of the Constellation Egg, is now dead. The egg was to come to us—or rather, to me—upon his death, but circumstances around his passing have caused more questions than answers, including why the contents of his will were suddenly changed just before his death. I am sending you the last known schematics of his estate. I do not know where he is keeping the egg. Sandi, that is for you to find out. You will also find an updated health certificate signed by Dr. Jon for Solomon to get him through customs."

Destin leaned forward across his desk, staring intently into the camera. Dorothy felt the hairs on her neck stand on end. "Get the egg and get out. I have no way to get to you if you are compromised, so your cover is completely your own. Be safe, foxes, and good luck."

The screen went black, and they heard a strange popping sound from the tablet. Sandi flipped the device over again, pulling off the back panel. A putrid smell filled the room, making Solomon jump from the couch and begin rubbing his face with his paws. The chip Sandi had placed in the tablet fell smoldering to the floor.

FOUR

SOLOMON CAREFULLY APPROACHED THE DESTROYED microchip, lifting a paw to bat at the thin line of smoke that rose into the air. Sandi leaned down and grabbed the chip in a handkerchief. The little cat continued to stare at the spot where the chip had lain, his nostrils flaring. He sneezed, rubbed his nose, and jumped into Dorothy's lap.

"Well, that was... different," Dorothy said, scratching Solomon behind the ears.

"I assume you mean Destin's briefing and not your cat's sneeze," said Sandi with the faintest grin.

Dorothy smiled, feeling some of the tension that had built during Destin's message subside. She reached for the envelope of papers that sat on the table between them. Handing the blueprint schematics of Grigory Alexeev's estate to Sandi, she sifted through the rest of the papers.

A short biography of Grigory and pictures of his family were all that remained.

"There's nothing about the egg in here," said Dorothy, peering in the envelope.

Sandi looked up from the schematics, his brow furrowed in concentration. "Destin said Grigory's family had kept the egg safe for years. I wonder why it didn't get passed down again."

Dorothy looked at Grigory's biography. "It looks like most his family are either in the military or are… veterinarians? That might have something to do with it. No obvious heir whom he could trust that wasn't connected to the Russian government, or who had any knowledge of such sensitive matters." She unfolded a particularly thick piece of paper and her eyes widened. "I think this is his death certificate."

Sandi set his blueprints aside and leaned forward.

"I can't read Russian," she said.

"Here, let me." Sandi pulled his phone from his pocket, holding out a hand for the paper. He snapped a picture of the certificate in question and went to work. He scrolled back and forth on his phone, scribbling notes with his stylus and pushing buttons with expertly deft fingers. Finally, he handed the document to Dorothy and leaned back.

"His time of death was less than an hour before Destin contacted me."

"What?" Dorothy asked. "How?"

"It says his cause of death was from old age."

"Could he have known he was going to die and contacted Destin?"

Sandi pressed his hands together, and Dorothy was sure his mind was spinning with as many thoughts as her own. It was the same exact diagnosis her father had been given, one that was at first dismissed, but later she'd learned was very unusual.

"I don't think there's a way to know until we get over there, but, as Destin said, we must be careful. If our mission is to get the egg and get out, it may be too dangerous to investigate Grigory's death any further."

Dorothy sighed and felt Solomon's toes curl reassuringly against her leg. "So, what *is* our cover for getting the egg?"

Sandi picked up his phone again and handed it to Dorothy. The smiling face of a very young Grigory dressed in a military uniform stared back at her. She scrolled down and read the broken translation of his obituary.

"Grigory was an officer during WWII," Sandi said, "where he was stationed in China. My father told us stories of Russian soldiers who fought the Japanese during the Second Sino-Japanese War. It would not be difficult to convince Grigory's family that our fathers knew each other in that war."

"And that you are coming to pay your respects," Dorothy finished with a nod. "What about me?"

Sandi tapped the metal cuff on his ear. "You're my interpreter," he said with another grin.

Dorothy laughed, making Solomon stand in her lap and nuzzle her chin. "But I don't speak Mandarin or Russian. How can I convince the family I'm interpreting their Russian into Mandarin? And wouldn't it be a little strange if I can understand Russian, but not speak it?"

Sandi nodded. "You are as astute as your father. But the cuff already has that well at hand. Do you see my lips moving as if I am speaking English?"

Dorothy sat straighter. "Yes. I—I didn't notice before, but…"

"The Babel artifact can alter the perception of those whom you are speaking to. You would still be able to understand me, and I you, if only one of us were wearing the artifact. If they believe you are speaking Russian, then you will appear and sound as if you are speaking Russian."

"And if they believe I'm translating what they've said into Mandarin, then they will see me speaking

Mandarin."

"Exactly."

"Well, that's quite a clever artifact." And a rather convenient one, she thought, a bit miffed Destin hadn't thought to loan it to her when she was in Iceland or Brazil. "I suppose that's it then. We're your fancy American interpreter and trusty feline sidekick."

She kissed Solomon's nose and shook her head. She was about to go on a dangerous mission with no guarantee of making it out alive. Her laugh belied the pounding of her heart. The fleeting thought that Destin was setting her up, that she had begun to dig too far and too deep into the truth about her father, nagged in the back of her mind. And the more she forced her smile, the harder her heart pounded.

Solomon turned toward the stair, his ears pricked up and his whiskers forward. He trilled quietly and jumped from Dorothy's lap, heading for the landing. A moment later, she heard a knock on the door, and the little cat trotted down the stairs. She heard the door open slightly, and a familiar voice drifted up to her.

"Ms. Claes?" said Aaron.

Dorothy let out a breath. She was more on edge than she'd realized. She took off her ear cuff and stood. "Aaron, what are you doing here?" she asked, standing at the top of the stair with her hands on her hips.

He kept the door open only a crack, wiggling his fingers through the space at Solomon. "I brought bagels," he declared triumphantly.

Dorothy padded down the steps and opened the door. Aaron looked back at her in surprise.

"You're feeling better," he said, smiling.

"I told you I was fine, dear."

Solomon mewed and took a running leap into Aaron's arms. He caught the cat, nearly dropping the bag of bagels he carried.

"Goodness, Solomon. Let the boy in," she said, stepping aside.

Aaron carried Solomon up the stairs, depositing the bagels on the kitchen counter, then tossing the jingle ball that sat beside the cat's food dish. He watched Solomon chase the ball across the sitting room and stiffened when he saw Sandi. The old man stood, and both bowed to each other in greeting.

"*Zǎoshang hǎo,*" said Aaron, making Dorothy pause halfway up the stairs.

"Ah, *tóngxué nǐ hǎo*, Aaron." Sandi tapped his watch and raised his eyebrow.

Aaron glanced at the clock on the kitchen wall. "Oh! It's, uh... *shà... shàngwǔ hǎo!*"

Sandi beamed, clapping his hands and bowing his head.

"I didn't know you spoke Mandarin," said Dorothy with a baited whisper.

"Oh, not really. Mr. Sandi taught me a few phrases a while ago. When I heard he was coming, I tried to brush up on some before coming over."

"Which, I told you, you didn't have to do," Dorothy scolded, pinching Aaron's cheek. He bit his lip and shrugged.

"Like I said, I had a coupon."

"Mhmm." Dorothy raised her own eyebrow at him and began unpacking the bag of bagels and cream cheese. "I'm glad you came," she said, patting his shoulder.

"Yeah?" Aaron tossed Solomon's ball again, and the little cat scampered across the floor, kinked tail flicking in the air as he tried to regain his balance, but instead, ran headlong into the armchair.

"Mr. Sandi needs a hand with a project. I'll be gone for a few days."

"I can watch Solomon for you," Aaron said, not bothering to stifle his laugh at the little cat.

"Oh, he's… he's coming with me," Dorothy said.

"Oh," Aaron replied dejected. "I'll watch the shop. Don't worry." He knelt, quietly reassuring Solomon's bruised ego and scratching his ears.

"Dorothy," Sandi called from the other room,

waving a piece of paper at her.

Dorothy patted Aaron's shoulder again as she crossed to the living room, turning her back to the young man so she could clip on the ear cuff without him seeing. She accepted the papers. It was their plane tickets. Her eyes scanned the tiny print, then widened. Their flight left that evening.

"Are you serious?" Dorothy cried.

"What?" Aaron asked.

Dorothy handed the paper back to Sandi, who tucked it into the envelope before Aaron could dare a glance.

"Oh, our flight leaves sooner than we thought," she said.

"I'll call a cab for you." Aaron had already pulled his phone out of his pocket.

A numbness suddenly filled her. Guilt and confusion. Should she tell him? What would happen to Aaron if Destin *was* sending her to her death? She watched Solomon rub against the young man's shins, then drop his favorite mousie at his feet. She took a deep breath and headed toward her bedroom.

The door snapped shut behind her, and for a moment, she heard Solomon paw at the gap beneath. She ignored him, covering the distance of the dark room to the closet. In a dilapidated envelope on the top shelf was a stack of documents. She pulled them down, sifting through until she found the will her lawyer had drawn up for her last year.

I devise, bequeath and give my antique shop, Richard's Anecdotes, to Aaron Williams.

"May he know the love of family wherever his travels take him," she read aloud.

FIVE

SOLOMON SHIFTED IN HIS CARRIER BENEATH the airline seat as the plane took off. Dorothy had waited until the last possible moment to force him in. Luckily, he hadn't protested much, but she could tell he was intentionally flopping from side to side into her heels to make his displeasure known.

"Settle down," she whispered, nudging him through the cloth carrier. She heard him give a pitiful mew, then turn in a circle and lie down. She was trying to be patient with him, as she was sure he was just as tired and frustrated as she was. Their flight from Boston to L.A. had gone smoothly, but their connecting flight to St. Petersburg had been delayed by two hours. She was sure the poor cat was starving by now, but he would have to wait to eat. She wasn't about to clean up any accidents that might occur–from either end of the disgruntled feline.

Sandi chuckled beside her. "He is a special one," he whispered.

"He's something," Dorothy replied, tucking her cane between their seats and pulling out her tablet.

She pulled up the pictures and biographies of Grigory's family, determined to memorize them before they landed. Sandi had the brilliant idea to take pictures of the documents Destin had sent them before they left the apartment. Once they landed, Sandi would wipe their devices, which also meant losing her connection to The Fox's Den.

Grigory had a small family. One son, one daughter, three grandchildren and one great-grand daughter.

The great-granddaughter, Maya, was of no consequence. She was in her tenth year of secondary school and only sixteen years old. Her mother, Tatiana, Grigory's eldest grandchild, was a veterinarian like her mother, Vera.

She flipped through the biographies, past the two grandsons in various military positions, past the younger brother who had retired from the military some time ago. He looked nearly on his deathbed himself.

She sighed and leaned back in her seat. Sandi sat beside her, his eyes closed and hands searching the air before him. She furrowed her brow, concerned the situation from the airport still had him shaken. Apparently, the number four was a superstitious number to the Chinese. Poor Sandi nearly had a heart attack when he saw Flight 444 was their plane. Luckily, it turned out to be a mistake on the departure board, but the situation had left the old man uneasy. She looked down and saw the estate schematics on Sandi's phone. Relieved, she turned her attention back to Solomon's tantrum.

A gentle BING sounded over the loudspeaker, and the Russian-accented voice of the captain followed. "*Zdravstvujtye*, passengers. This is your captain. We apologize for the delay in your flight, but we are underway with mostly clear skies ahead of us. Thank you for your patience and enjoy your flight."

The seatbelt light above the cockpit door turned off, and a heavily pregnant woman across the aisle made a mad dash for the bathroom. Solomon huffed and mewed from under the seat again, and Dorothy reached under, pulling the carrier onto her lap.

"Stay quiet, and you can sit on my lap, okay?" she whispered, unzipping the top flap. Solomon poked his nose out and graciously accepted her pets. The carrier was designed to look like a purse. She didn't use it much but figured the less attention she could draw, the better. Unlike her last cases with Solomon, where his presence had been something she could use to her advantage, this time, she needed to blend in as much as possible. The only problem was, the purse-carrier was smaller than Solomon was used to on long trips.

The little cat pushed his cold nose into her palm, and she felt him begin to purr. He kneaded into her legs through the cushion of the carrier, and Dorothy relaxed, tucking the tablet back into her real purse. Research could wait.

The pregnant woman walked back down the aisle, holding her belly as she swayed and sighed. She sat in her seat again and turned to smile at Dorothy. Solomon poked his head out of the bag, looked at the woman, then popped back in again.

The woman's smile deepened. She winked at Dorothy and put her finger to her lips.

Dorothy smiled back. "I thought one shouldn't fly when they were so far along," she said, rubbing Solomon's chin.

The woman nodded. "Extenuating circumstances," she replied. "And you can do anything if you have enough money."

Dorothy raised her eyebrows and nodded in agreement.

The woman reached across the aisle as much as she

could, extending a hand to Dorothy.

"I'm Mary Ann," she said.

"Dorothy," she replied, accepting her hand.

"My great-aunt's name was Dorothy," Mary Ann mused.

"It used to be a popular name."

"Well, I think it still should be. Though this one, he'll be named after my brother." She rubbed her belly, then winced shifting in her seat. "So, what brings you to Russia?"

"A funeral, unfortunately," Dorothy replied.

"Oh, I'm so sorry. Was… was it sudden?"

"Um, a bit," said Dorothy. "I'm Mr. Sandi's interpreter." She gestured toward Sandi, who had fallen asleep beside her. "It was his father's friend. Mr. Sandi wishes to pay his respects, and, well, here I am."

"Here you are," Mary Ann said with a coy grin, "and here is your cat."

"Emotional support animal. Mr. Sandi suffers from severe PTSD."

Mary Ann gave an empathetic smile, though Dorothy noticed her eyelids began to look heavy.

"Well, I think Mr. Sandi has the right idea," said Mary Ann. "It's going to be a long flight."

Dorothy cleared her throat and nodded, feeling a chill run the length of her body. Lying was becoming so easy, so second nature to her. She didn't like it. Solomon pushed into her hand, which had remained resting inside the carrier. At least he would still love her no matter how many lies she told.

$\mathscr{S}$IX

"YOU MUST VISIT THE HERMITAGE MUSEUM. THEY have a beautiful cat colony. You would love it." Mary Ann adjusted the bag on her shoulder, the contents rattling inside sounding surprisingly heavy for a near-full-term woman to be lugging around.

Dorothy shifted Solomon's bag on her own shoulder and leaned into her cane. The change in altitude had somehow set off her knee again, causing it to throb. She stood just outside the Pulkovo Airport, waiting for Sandi to finish wiping their devices of any incriminating Foxes information.

"I remember it from my travels with my late husband. It's quite interesting," Dorothy said, looking anxiously at the line of doors behind her. For a moment, her stomach sank. Her mind raced with the reasons Sandi was taking so long—thoughts of betrayal and... She pushed them away, turning back to Mary Ann with a forced smile.

A taxi pulled up to the curb and immediately popped the trunk. Mary Ann lugged the bag inside with ease before slamming the trunk shut.

"It *is* very interesting. Have a good trip!" She gave Dorothy a wink, then climbed into the back of the cab, her door barely closed before it sped off into the gray horizon.

Dorothy watched her go, her mind contemplating a dozen thoughts at once. She shook her head. It was just nerves, she told herself. The case was getting to her. Perhaps she needed to speak with Destin about taking a break.

The door opened behind her, and a throng of people poured out. She waited, fidgeting with the strap of Solomon's carrier, until she saw Sandi bringing up the rear.

"Done," he said, patting the side of his briefcase.

"I think we should drop our things at the hotel first," Dorothy suggested.

"We'll be cutting it close for the funeral if we do." Sandi glanced at his watch, the wrinkles around his eyes deepening.

"I know, but we can't haul our luggage around while on a case. It'll only get in the way."

Sandi nodded begrudgingly as the mass of people around them began to thin, climbing into taxis and shuttle buses. They waved down a cab and piled in, urging the driver to hurry.

Dorothy clutched to the safety assist handle with one hand, the other clinging to Solomon's carrier between her and Sandi. She had forgotten how terrible St. Petersburg traffic was. She gritted her teeth, feeling more and more like she was driving with her nephew, Craig, by the minute. Sandi gripped the handle assist on his side. He gave Dorothy a worried glance as the car slammed on its brakes only to suddenly speed off a moment later. He looked dangerously green.

They pulled off the highway and onto the streets of St. Petersburg. The traffic didn't lessen, however. Cars were packed into every place that could be used as a parking space. Vehicles would stop for minutes at a time while drivers fought to get out of and then into a parking space. Dorothy tried to ignore the endless onslaught of blaring horns and the occasional expletive from their driver. She assumed they were swear words though the Babel ear cuff had a few interesting translations. Instead, she stared at the tall buildings that surrounded them, remembering the times she and Frank had walked these streets, trying to decide whether the iron gates of an estate were from the Neo-Classical or Baroque period.

The buildings of St. Petersburg hearkened back to a time of grandeur and excess interspersed with everything from florists and banks to coffee shops and cell phone providers. They slowed as they approached another traffic jam, and Solomon huffed and meowed in annoyance.

Sandi checked his watch again, then grabbed for the handle assist as the car took off unexpectedly. "We're not going to make it if we stop," he said.

Solomon mewed pitifully. Dorothy had given him a litter box in the airport bathroom when they'd exited the plane. He was being melodramatic as usual, though she couldn't blame him for wanting to get out of the cramped carrier. She nodded to Sandi, who leaned forward and directed the driver to change course to Grigory's residence. Since she wore the second ear cuff, she heard his words through the strange whooshing sound as her native language, not the language Sandi was impressing upon the driver. It was a complicated artifact, and she was beginning to understand why Destin did not release them so easily.

They drove—if one could call it driving—for another half hour before turning down several side streets and away from the town center. They pulled up to a set of heavy metal gates where a tall, thin security guard stood sentry.

"Name?" he asked as Dorothy rolled down her back window, looking down at the tiny clipboard he pulled from his jacket.

"I don't think we're on the list," Dorothy said, praying the Babel ear cuff was working.

The man raised a discerning eyebrow and peered into the vehicle at Sandi.

"I'm Mr. Sandi's translator. His father served in the Sino-Japanese War with Grigory. He's come to pay his respects on his father's behalf."

Solomon meowed again between them, and Dorothy nudged the carrier.

A car horned wailed, making them all jump. The guard's hand flew to his hip, where Dorothy was sure a gun was holstered.

"What's going on?" a woman called. Dorothy heard the lilt of Russian behind her translation like a backup harmony in a piece of music.

"They're not on the list, Tatiana," the guard shouted back.

Dorothy leaned out the window and watched as a woman in a tight black dress and matching black veil stepped from the car behind them. She was tall and looked barely over thirty. But if this was Tatiana Denisnovna Anatakova, she was Grigory's granddaughter, and was easily in her mid-forties. Her long, platinum blonde hair was pulled back into a loose bun, and her figure was slim but fit.

"*Mamochka*," she whispered to someone in the car. "I'll handle this." She adjusted her veil and trudged up the drive, her shoulders squared with a practiced confidence. "Maksim, we're going to be late," she quipped. She turned to Dorothy, who still sat within the vehicle. "I'm sorry about this."

"Tatiana," the guard reiterated, "they are not on the list." He held up the clipboard to her.

Tatiana rolled her eyes, dropping any semblance of formality and poise that came with her station in society. "Oh, to hell with the list! How did you know my grandfather?" she asked Dorothy.

"Mr. Sandi's father served with him in the war," Dorothy repeated.

The woman gestured toward Dorothy. "There, you see? Now, for the love of Russia, open the damn gates."

"Yes, Tatiana."

Maksim shoved the clipboard back into his jacket pocket, then typed in a code hidden in a stone pillar behind him. He stared suspiciously as the gates creaked and slid apart with a quiet little beep. Tatiana gave a reassuring nod to Dorothy and headed back to her own vehicle.

The taxi driver pulled up to the front entrance and popped the trunk before he put the car into park. Sandi seemed to lurch out of the car, and Dorothy was close behind, Solomon's carrier slung over her shoulder. They pulled their suitcases out of the back and watched the driver pull away as Tatiana's car pulled up behind them.

A teenage girl was the first to step out. She held out a hand helping a woman close to Dorothy's age from the vehicle. Both had the same thin nose and slightly crooked smile. This must have been Grigory's daughter, Vera, and his great-granddaughter, Maya.

Tatiana closed the door on the other side, nodding to Maya approvingly over the top of the car with the same crooked smile. "Come on," she said to Dorothy and Sandi, "They won't start without us, but I'll never hear the end of it from Yury if we hold things up."

She grabbed the handle of Sandi's suitcase and carried it up the stone steps, past Vera and Maya, and through the double front doors. Dorothy barely had time to catch Sandi's eye. He shrugged and followed Tatiana, taking two steps at a time. Solomon mewed pitifully from under her arm, heaving himself against the side of the carrier in protest.

"Oh, all right," Dorothy breathed, setting the bag on the ground. She pulled his leash from a side pocket and unzipped the top of the carrier, clipping the leash on before he jumped out.

Tatiana's daughter gasped from halfway up the steps, and her grandmother turned to look.

"Ah, a little feline treasure," she said with a smile. "My father would be pleased." She patted the girl's arm, this time taking the lead up the steps.

"But, *Babushka*," the girl mutter before stepping inside the front doors.

Solomon shook, stretched and trotted up the stairs without prompt, his head and bent tail held high. Dorothy gathered her own suitcase, dragging it up the steps behind her cat as quickly as her knees would allow. Sandi waited for them at the top and held the door open.

"Thanks," Dorothy said, then barely stifled a gasp.

Grigory's estate was an almost perfect preservation of the 17th century Baroque design. Not surprising for the area, but the preservation was astounding to her curator eye. The hall was lined with small alcoves, their curved borders and domed ceilings framing individual murals on each wall. The winding stair on the other side was wide enough for four people at least. Its carved banister was in near mint condition, as was the marble tile they stood upon.

Tatiana emerged from a side room, a smile spreading

across her face as she stared at Dorothy. "Beautiful, isn't it?" she asked.

Solomon's ears pricked forward at the sound of her voice, and he immediately approached her.

"Well, hello there," she said, bending down to pet the little cat. She ran her hand along his back and up his tail as Solomon rubbed against her shins. "You've been through it all, haven't you?" she cooed. "I thought I heard a cat, but then I'm always hearing animals."

"Do you work with animals?" Dorothy asked, eyeing Solomon as he continued to accost Tatiana's legs with his face. She gestured at the woman's hands, the faint scars of her profession answering before she could.

The woman nodded. "I do. Most of the women in my family have gone into veterinary medicine. We have quite a history of caring for the animals of Russia." She motioned toward the motifs on the walls of the alcoves.

Dorothy looked closer. All of them depicted animals, and all bore the Alexeev family crest—an axe and a lion. Along the top of one painting was written 'S Rioghal Mo Dhream. Royal is my blood.

The sound of hymnal song rose from the room behind Tatiana.

"Come," she whispered, holding out her hand to Sandi. "I will help you pay your respects to my grandfather."

Several awkward seconds passed in which Dorothy continued to stare at the entrance hall around her. Sandi cleared his throat, bringing her thoughts back.

"Are you going to translate for me?" he murmured. Dorothy could hear the Mandarin underlying the English, and she hoped Mandarin was what Grigory's family heard as well. That's when the realization struck her.

"Oh! Yes!" Dorothy exclaimed. She quickly feigned translating, her cheeks flushing with embarrassment.

Sandi played the part perfectly. His eyes lit up in mock understanding as he bowed to Tatiana and allowed her to lead him away. Dorothy scooped Solomon into her arms and followed close behind, the pressures of the mission barely keeping her on task as the history of the house called to her.

As Dorothy rounded the corner, she saw the furniture in what would have been the drawing room cleared away, leaving plenty of room for the family to gather around Grigory's casket. The crowd wasn't as large as Dorothy expected, but it still filled most of the room. They circled the casket counterclockwise, leaning in to kiss the man's forehead and lay flowers upon his chest.

Dorothy stood at the back of the room with Solomon

in her arms, observing the funerary rituals with baited curiosity. She watched as Tatiana found her daughter and pointed to a small box in the corner. The girl rolled her eyes but obliged her mother, pocketing her cell phone and weaving her way through the crowd. Tatiana made exaggerated gestures to Sandi, doing her best to broach the supposed linguistic barrier, and the two joined the gathering of people that continued to circle the casket, singing hymns in Russian as they went.

Maya wove her way through the crowd of people and approached Dorothy with two lit candles. She hesitated, her eyes darting between the cat in Dorothy's arms and the lit candles in her hand.

"Oh, I'm... uh..." she stammered.

Her hesitation needed no translation. Dorothy set Solomon at her feet, gathering the excess leash in her hand. But he didn't bolt. He stood stiffly, staring and sniffing the air in front of the girl. Dorothy had never seen him act like this before. He wasn't afraid, but he was certainly on high alert. Maya stared back, seeming just as transfixed on the little cat as he was on her. With a tentative step, Solomon approached her as if he were hunting prey. His whiskers tickled her bare legs, and the girl gasped. Finally, and without warning, Solomon flopped across her feet.

"You can pet him if you like," Dorothy said, reaching

for the two candles still in Maya's hand.

Maya hesitated, though her eyes shone with delight. She looked over her shoulder, then thrust the candles at Dorothy before joining Solomon on the floor. Carefully, she reached out a hand, pulling away at the last moment when Solomon sniffed her, before petting his head gingerly.

"What's his name?" she whispered, looking over her shoulder again.

"Solomon," Dorothy replied, loosening her grip on the leash ever-so-slightly. "What's your name?" she asked, hoping she had identified the girl correctly.

"Maya," she confirmed, taking her eyes off Solomon only to check the crowd every so often. He wiggled and draped himself across her lap, making her giggle with delight. "What happened to his tail?"

Dorothy took advantage of Maya's distraction to scan the room intently for any signs of a keypad or secret door. Nothing in the home's restoration looked out of place. "He was in a fight with a very large cat," she said.

"Aw! You poor thing!" Maya cried, pulling Solomon into her arms. The little cat melted into the affection with utter glee. "*Praded* would have loved you."

For a moment, Maya's face fell. She pulled Solomon into a brief hug before releasing him.

"*Praded* is your... great-grandfather?"

Maya loosening her hold on Solomon. "When we moved here, I didn't know anyone. *Praded* was my best friend."

"You must miss him terribly," Dorothy said gently.

Maya hung her head. "He called me his little guardian. I took care of him, and—"

"Maya!" came a man's harsh voice. A white-haired man in a highly decorated military uniform strode toward them, his eyes narrowed, and the lines around his mouth deepening. He grabbed Maya's shoulder, dragging her to her feet. "Get off the floor," he seethed, the underlying whooshing sound of the Babel cuff translator taking on a higher pitch in Dorothy's ear. "What are you doing? Are you mad? You could get hurt!"

"I was just—"

"You will pay your respects to your great-grandfather, not roll on the floor like a dog."

Maya's lip trembled. She hung her head and bustled off into the crowd that seemed to be trying to ignore the commotion.

The man rounded on Dorothy, and she saw Solomon bristle at him. "Who are you?"

"Dorothy Fennec," she replied, flashing an unintimidated smile. "I'm Mr. Sandi's translator."

"I might have guessed you were the one Maksim informed me of. I'm warning you now, this is a sacred tradition, and I will not have you make a mockery of my family."

"What's going on? Yury?" Tatiana joined them, her arm still intertwined with Sandi's.

"I found your daughter on the floor with this filthy animal," Yury said. He thrust his chin at Solomon, though his eyes flicked upward at Dorothy.

"Filthy animal? Now, I'm sure I know far more about cats than you do, and I can assure you neither he nor his owner are filthy in any way."

"Maya could have been hurt, Tatiana. They don't belong here."

"They have as much right as anyone else to pay their respects to *Dedushka*." The man opened his mouth to speak, but Tatiana cut him off. "Even the cat."

"Yury?" said a woman's voice behind them.

"*Mamochka*," Tatiana said, stepping aside for her mother. "This is Mr. Sandi and his translator. Mr. Sandi's father served in the war with *Dedushka*. I'm sorry, I didn't catch your name?"

"Dorothy Fennec," Dorothy said, holding out her hand. She despised her alias name of Fanny Fennec, and preferred to use her given first name, despite Destin's insistence otherwise.

"Vera Grigorevna Borisovna," the old woman said, holding her hand out to Sandi. "A pleasure to meet you, Mr. Sandi. And I thought I saw your feline companion outside." She smiled down at Solomon, who was now sitting firmly atop Dorothy's feet as the crowd grew around them.

Sandi took Vera's hand between his and bowed. "He is my emotional support animal," he said, and Dorothy quickly pretended to translate for him.

Yury rolled his eyes. "An animal does not belong at a funeral."

"And where are you staying?" Vera asked, ignoring her brother.

"The Dostoevsky hotel," Dorothy said.

Vera sneered and waved a hand in the air. "Oh, no. No. That won't do. No. Tatiana, find Karina and tell her to fix up two of the servants' quarters rooms." She turned back to Dorothy and Sandi, her hand finally released. "You must stay here."

"Oh, I - um… we couldn't poss—"

Tatiana waved her hand like her mother, cutting Dorothy off. "We insist."

Despite his dominating stature and intimidating uniform, Yury couldn't have been less in control. The women of the house had swooped in with their traditions of hospitality, undermining any authority

Dorothy originally thought he may have held being the eldest son of Grigory. His face was bright red, and a vein was popping along his forehead.

Dorothy feigned translation again to Sandi.

"It would make searching for the egg easier," Sandi replied.

"We would love to stay. Thank you." Dorothy and Sandi bowed in unison to their new hosts. She hoped the gesture wasn't too over the top, but rather made their cover more believable if she picked up some of her would-be-client's mannerisms.

With a patronizing smile, Vera turned back to her brother, gently patting the lapel of his uniform. "You should be paying your respects to *Otets*."

Yury stormed off into the crowd with Vera close on his heels.

"The ceremonies will finish here soon, and then we'll head to the cemetery. I'll make sure you have transportation." Tatiana smiled, though the emotion did not rise to her eyes. She rejoined the crowd of people circling and singing around her grandfather, a bit more tension riding in her shoulders.

"Well?" Dorothy whispered to Sandi. "Did you see or overhear anything while you were over there?"

Sandi stepped closer to her, though he did not break from examining the crowd. "No, and I'm beginning to think it may be futile to try anything while the ceremonies are going on."

"Agreed," Dorothy whispered, wiggling her toes beneath Solomon to get the circulation going again. "But we can't stay long after things have ended. It will look suspicious."

"There is a meal planned after the graveside service. I may be able to sneak away then."

Dorothy took a deep breath. This was the first mission she felt she may fail. By now, she always had a lead, someone she could talk to, or simply follow. Solomon rubbed his cheek against her shin and lay across her feet. She pushed away the thought that failure of this mission might mean her death. Sighing, Solomon closed his eyes. At least someone was at ease around here. She adjusted the candle in her hand and leaned more into the cane in the other. Her knees were no longer bothering her, but of a wave of exhaustion reverberated through her body.

"Jet lag is a terrible bother at our age," Sandi whispered beside her.

"And a terrible bother to this mission."

"We'll figure it out," Sandi assured her, and began scanning the room once more.

SEVEN

WHEN DOROTHY RETURNED TO THE ESTATE, she was more thankful than ever for her cane. The trip to the grave site alone had taken a half hour, and the service lasted for another hour. Her only saving grace was a small nap she had snuck in during the trip to and from the cemetery, though it did little to refresh her.

Her and Sandi's things had been taken to the renovated third-floor servants' quarters before they left. She had begrudgingly left Solomon locked away with his litter box, food and all the toys she'd managed to shove into his travel bag before leaving her apartment—a few of which she was sure Aaron had snuck in when she hadn't been looking. She leaned against the wide banister of the stair, admiring the chandelier medallion centered on the ceiling above when a plump woman in khaki scrubs and an apron approached.

"Madam," she said, her Russian words lost in the background whirlwind of the Babel artifact, "you may take the elevator." She gestured toward a door Dorothy had thought was a closet when she'd first entered the grand foyer.

"Elevator?" Dorothy asked.

The woman nodded. She slid open the door, revealing a service elevator. Dorothy stood straighter, wondering when it had been installed and what architecture had been sacrificed for it. And also wondering why Yury hadn't mentioned it earlier when she had to lug Solomon up three flights of stairs before they left for the grave site. She stepped carefully inside, and the woman leaned in, gesturing to a panel on the right.

"Your room is on the third floor," she said, pointing to the series of buttons.

There appeared to be access to only four floors. They currently sat on the first, as indicated by the small glowing light beside the button for One.

"The second floor is the family's apartments," the woman continued, pointing.

"What's this one?" Dorothy asked, pointing at button with a Russian letter she couldn't read.

"That is the basement."

Dorothy's heart skipped a beat. Her grip tightened on the handle of her cane, but she kept her composure. "Oh," she feigned nonchalance. "What's down there?"

The woman shrugged. "It's storage, mostly. Furniture, the wine cellar. Also shelter from war. Anyway, make sure you secure the gate before pushing the buttons. It won't go if it isn't locked."

She pulled a collapsible gate across the entrance to the elevator and flashed a smile. "Third floor," she reminded Dorothy, holding up three fingers.

"Third floor," Dorothy repeated and pushed the button.

The elevator jolted, and Dorothy heard the mechanical sound of gears as it rose into the air. She had ridden in old elevators before, but it still unnerved her to see the inner walls of the elevator shaft whiz by. At least they weren't on the fourth floor. Sandi would have rather slept in the garden, she was sure. With more grace than when it had started, the elevator eased to a stop with a little bounce. She slid the grate open and turned the handle for the door.

Where the halls of the second floor looked down on the level below, the third floor was completely closed off from the rest of the home. No elaborate crown moldings or Baroque art adorned the walls. The ceilings were low in comparison, decorated with plain light fixtures that gave off a certain high-pitched buzz when Dorothy stood beneath them. Even the door frames were square and straight, unlike the rounded or scalloped ones on the main floor.

She closed the door to the elevator behind her and immediately stopped. A door handle rattled somewhere down the hall. She adjusted her grip on her cane, ready to use it to defend herself if necessary, and crept toward the sound. As she drew closer, the rattling stopped, and she heard the mournful yowl of Solomon from behind one of the doors.

"Oh, for heaven's sake." She leaned her cane against the wall and opened the door, immediately scooping the little cat into her arms as he made a bolt for it. "No, you don't."

Solomon struggled only long enough to flip himself around and hug Dorothy's neck. She hugged him back, picking up her cane and heading into the room.

It was larger than what would have been typical of a servant's quarters, or so it seemed. Four or five bunk beds would have been forced into the space during the 1700s, but her single bed made the room seem spacious. The renovations had turned what would have been plain, whitewashed walls into period reproduction wallpaper, and the accents of rich wood on the end table and wardrobe completed the simple aesthetic. Dorothy felt more at home than she had on any recent mission, the designs bringing back memories of her time at the Boston Museum.

She deposited Solomon on the bed, turning back to the door. The handle was an ornately decorated lever style. Not period, Dorothy noted, but still Solomon's favorite type as he could easily open them. She glanced around the room, looking for something to tie the handle to as an anchor, but the room was rather bare.

"I guess I'll have to keep you occupied then," she said, and Solomon immediately jumped into her arms.

There was a gentle knock on the inner door. Solomon leapt from her shoulder, using her chest as a launching pad, and sniffed at the space beneath the door.

"Fennec?" She heard Sandi's voice through the artifact.

Dorothy opened the door, and Solomon immediately circled Sandi's ankles. The tiny man reached down, and the little cat jumped onto his shoulders.

"Solomon!" Dorothy scolded.

"He's fine," Sandi said, holding up a hand to stop her from grabbing the cat. "He's been cooped up for longer than any cat should be."

"There are worse things he could do to protest, I suppose," said Dorothy, and held the door wide for Sandi.

"How was your ride with Vera?" Dorothy asked, taking a seat on the bed.

"Uneventful," Sandi said as Solomon paced back and forth on his shoulders. "She didn't speak with Yury at all. What about Tatiana and Maya?"

Dorothy shook her head. "Not much. Maya mentioned wanting to visit her father, and Tatiana said she would reach out to him. But nothing, I think, to do with the artifact. But I may have found something back here at the house."

Sandi beamed, shifting Solomon's position. The little cat placed his paws on either side of the man's head and began licking his thinning hair.

"There's a basement level, and you can access it from the elevator."

Sandi's eyes lit up at Dorothy's words. "They're laying out the mourning meal as we speak," he said, graciously ignoring Solomon's grooming. "After tomorrow, we won't have a reason to stay here."

"I know." Dorothy leaned over and peeled Solomon off her fellow agent, much to the little cat's annoyance. "Our time is limited. If the basement is a dead end, have you found any other potential leads?"

Sandi shifted uncomfortably, squinting his eyes in frustration. "The style of architecture of the house lends itself well to hidden panels and doors. But,"—he paused long enough to toss the jingle ball Solomon had dropped at his feet—"I think I may have something. One of the paintings in the entrance hall has a phrase painted above it."

"*'S Rioghal Mo Dhream*," said Dorothy. "Royal is my blood."

Sandi chuckled. "I should have known the art historian could read Latin. Anyway, I did eventually figure out its meaning."

"You think the vault may be through there?"

"That is my guess. If I recall the blueprints correctly, there is an empty space behind that wall, which is probably why they had room to put in a small elevator."

"But before the elevator, what would it have been used for? And what about the rest of the space?"

"Exactly," Sandi said, bowing his head. "I should be able to find this out easily enough. *If* I can get away during the meal."

Dorothy thought for a moment, ignoring Solomon's pawing at her leg until one of his claws poked through her socks. She tossed the toy he had brought her and furrowed her brow.

"Tatiana said something to me earlier. She said her family has a history of caring for the animals of Russia. Not just caring for animals. It was *how* she said it. I have a hunch that her ancestors may have cared for the Tsar's pets."

"Which would have included Alexei Romanov's cat."

Dorothy nodded. "Perhaps she knows more. She certainly seems the talkative type."

"If you can keep the family distracted with talking about their history and connections to the Tsars, it should give me enough time to investigate those facades."

Solomon deposited his toy beside his water dish and made a running jump into Dorothy's lap. She scratched his ears until he curled between her and Sandi, purring loudly.

"Is that it, then?" she asked. "Is that our plan?"

Sandi shrugged. "Seems to be."

Dorothy furrowed her brow again. "It feels too easy."

"With your history of encounters, I'm sure it does! But I can assure you, not all missions are as exciting."

"Were you ever on any missions with my father?"

Sandi sat straighter, and Solomon's purring stuttered. "Of course." A smile spread across his face. "I'll never forget the time he thought he could smuggle a terracotta soldier out under a tarp."

Dorothy laughed, but it was short-lived. "Did...

Was there ever anything odd about him?"

"Odd? Other than his plan for the terracotta soldier actually working, I'm not sure what you mean."

"I don't know. Something different that set him apart from the other agents."

Stroking the little cat between them, Sandi sat quietly, thinking. "He was a very trusting man. But his instincts of whom to trust were always spot on. The trait seems to run in the family, or so I've heard."

Dorothy sighed. It wasn't the answer she had been hoping for, but then she wasn't sure what answer she had been expecting.

Sandi set a hand on her shoulder. "He was a wonderful man, and one of our best agents. You are continuing his legacy proudly."

He squeezed her shoulder, and Dorothy squeezed his hand back. "I just wish I knew what happened to him."

"We all do."

Dorothy turned so quickly, Solomon started, lifting his head and yawning widely up at her. She bit her lip, staring into Sandi's dark brown eyes. The note she had found in her father's vault came to her. Should she dare ask him? Her eyes glanced over the cuff on his ear. She couldn't risk that the artifact might be translating their conversations back to Destin, risking him finding out what she knew. Or, at least what she thought she knew. She still had no idea if it was a true lead or not.

With another sigh, she rose to her feet, still leaning on her cane to steady herself. "Well, let's go see if my instincts about Tatiana are as good as my father's."

&IGHT

THE ELEVATOR GLIDED TO A HALT AS IT SETTLED into place on the first floor. Sandi pushed aside the gate and held the door for Dorothy. She stepped out, pausing for a moment to listen at the banister of the winding stair. They had left Solomon in the room with a handful of treats behind the bathroom door in an attempt to keep him occupied. She didn't hear the rattle of the door handle or his distinct chirps whenever he found somewhere that echoed—like the hall of the servants' quarters.

Not entirely satisfied, she followed Sandi through the entrance hall. Both slowed as they passed the murals painted within the alcoves but continued toward the sound of crowds and cutlery. They entered another magnificent room, this one just as gilded and decorated as the rest of the home, though Dorothy saw evidence of peeling wallpaper and fading paint around the windows and trim. They stood in the doorway as Grigory's family filled their plates with food and sat around a large, antique dining table.

Vera spotted them first. "How are your rooms?" she asked.

"Lovely, thank you," Dorothy said, looking at the buffet of food and leaning nonchalantly into her cane until she remembered she was supposed to be Sandi's translator. She quickly pretended to translate, hoping the pause didn't seem too suspicious. He played along perfectly, smiling and bowing when appropriate.

"Good, very good. I've saved you a seat by Tatiana. I'm sure she'd love to hear stories about my father during the war, Mr. Sandi. Our family history is her passion."

Vera led them through the crowd with ease and indicated the last two untouched place settings.

Tatiana rose when she saw them, holding out her hand in greeting. "I'm so glad you decided to stay. Please, I'm sure you're starving after your trip."

As if on cue, Dorothy's stomach rumbled.

"Maya," Tatiana said as the girl scrolled through her cell phone. "Will you help Ms. Fennec and Mr. Sandi with their plates?"

Maya looked shyly up at the pair and nodded. She

picked up both plates, handing one each to Sandi and Dorothy, and joined the dwindling line of people at the buffet.

"Have you ever been to a *pominki*?" Maya asked.

Dorothy scratched at her ear cuff, wondering why it hadn't translated.

Maya must have sensed her hesitation and replied, "The mourning meal. It's the meal after a loved one's burial."

"Oh," said Dorothy. "Yes, well, not in Russia. We have something similar in America." She turned to Sandi, pretending to translate artifact must not have easy translations for such unique words, or titles when they were used as names of endearment, like when Tatiana referred to her mother as *Mamochka*.

"These are *kolyva*," Maya continued, indicating the array of domed cakes that were first in the long line of dishes. "It's sweet. Like a dessert."

"That sounds delicious," Dorothy said.

A faint smile crossed Maya's lips. "I made this one," she said, dishing out a piece to each before stepping farther down the line. She introduced them to other foods she said were typically served at a *pominki*, such as *blinis* and fish pies. But Grigory's family had not shied away from their wealthy roots, either. Tiny dishes of caviar sat beside the crackers and behind it was a mound of Kamchatka crab. They had spread out an entire smoked salmon on the table as if it were little more than bread and jam.

"Do you like salmon?" Maya murmured, and Dorothy caught more Russian within the translation than English.

"Yes," she said, holding out the plate.

"*Praded* loved salmon," she said, mounding their plates with the smoked meat. "Sometimes, we would sneak down to the kitchens at night and get into the jars of salmon caviar. It made *Babushka* so angry." She giggled, daring a glance at Vera, but her smile quickly faded.

Dorothy touched Maya's back. "You must miss him very much."

"He was my best friend. I only wish he would have finished teaching me—"

A strong arm pushed its way between the pair, and Maya jumped back as Yury wasted no time in filling his plate with fruit and crab. He stomped back to the table, not hiding his displeasure at their presence. He glared down the table as they took their seats, stopping only long enough to take a bite of food or a sip of his cocktail.

Maya seemed to shrink from him, hiding beside her mother as she picked at her food. Tatiana must have noticed her daughter's nervous energy. She squeezed her hand and glared back at Yury until the man finally looked away, though she kept an arm draped over the back of her daughter's chair.

"Your mother says you are the family historian," Dorothy said to Tatiana, trying to break the tension in the air.

Tatiana swallowed the last of her *kolyva* and dabbed the napkin at her mouth. "Well, I don't know about historian, but it's very interesting."

"I'm heading out," Sandi whispered to Dorothy and stood.

"Is he well?" Tatiana asked, glancing between the pair.

"Yes. He's just tired." Dorothy flashed a reassuring smile as Sandi made a series of deep bows to their guests and left. "Tell me, have your family always been veterinarians?"

Tatiana laughed, turning her attention back to Dorothy. "For the most part. We have served those in power of Russia for many years, both in the military and as support for their war animals."

"And this estate. Has your family always owned it?"

Tatiana blushed at the flattery, and Dorothy knew her distraction would hold for a little while. She only hoped it was long enough for Sandi to find something.

"It hasn't been easy. A house this large takes quite a bit of staff to upkeep, and of course the expense to maintain."

"*Mamochka's* been restoring the house so we can give tours and take in visitors," Maya chimed in, seeming to find her voice again.

"We have to stay alive and relevant," Tatiana whispered, grinning at her daughter. "You adapt or you die."

"Alexeevs don't adapt," Yury said, finishing off his drink and snapping his fingers at a passing staff member for another. "We have survived this long, and I have assured you we will survive this."

"You and your schemes, Yury," Vera chided. She had been sitting quietly across from Tatiana, and Dorothy had almost forgotten she was there.

"My *schemes* are what will save this family! Not some American tourist and a trip down memory lane!" Yury snatched the drink from the returning staffer and charged out of the room, leaving an awkward silence stretching from one end of the table to the other.

As the chatter picked up again, Vera leaned toward Dorothy. "You must excuse my brother. He is not taking our father's death well."

"I understand," Dorothy said. "I lost my own father not long ago. It's been over a year, but…"

"*Djadja* doesn't care about *Praded*," Maya seethed under her breath. "He just wants the money. He doesn't care about our responsibility."

Though she pretended not to hear her, Tatiana's gaze held her daughter for a moment. She set her napkin on her plate and pushed back her chair. "Would you like a tour?" she asked Dorothy. "It will give me some practice when we are finally ready to receive guests."

Dorothy glanced over her shoulder. Sandi hadn't been gone long. He might still be in the entrance hall, and she didn't want to risk having him caught. But if the artifact was linked to the Alexeevs' history, then a history lesson may very well be what she needed to solve the case. Besides, if Frank were still here, he wouldn't let her pass up an opportunity for a private tour.

She thought back to her first visit to Russia. Back to when Frank was still with her. It had been just after they adopted Solomon, though they had left him in their hotel room for much of their visit. She'd stood hand in hand with him in the St. Isaac's Cathedral. She'd wanted to stay at the back of the tour group, but Frank had insisted they go to the front.

"I want you to experience this with your heart," he had whispered to her, and Dorothy could almost feel his warm breath against her ear now. "Not through the heads of bored schoolgirls who don't even want to be here. Always at the front, my love."

And so he'd taken her hand, guiding her through the crowd to the front where a thin woman with short red hair had stood.

"And this is Anna Ivanovna, or Empress Anna," the thin woman had said. "She took the throne after Peter II, with a little help from members of the Supreme Privy Council, like Dmitry Golitsyn."

Dorothy set her own napkin on the table and rose. "That sounds wonderful."

Tatiana linked her arm through Dorothy's and led her not toward the entrance hall, but through a side room. This room was much smaller than most Dorothy had so far seen. It appeared to have once been a workroom. The floors were paved in cracking marble tiles, and along the wall were long, scrubbed wooden tables. They reminded her of the ones in her father's vault, but these held no magical artifacts, at least none so far as Dorothy could tell. Instead, pictures, stethoscopes, and old veterinary textbooks were laid out on display.

"This will be one of the first stops in the tour, but I haven't decided yet where to put everything, so I'm storing them here," Tatiana said.

"May I?" Dorothy asked.

Tatiana unlinked her arm and gestured toward

the tables. Dorothy stepped closer, her eyes roving carefully over each item as Tatiana spoke behind her.

"In the early 1800s, Nicholas Alexeev was admitted to Claude Bourgelat's first veterinary medicine school in Lyon, France. This was the beginning of a long line of animal caretakers and trainers from the Alexeev family in service to the Russian aristocracy. This is him here." She stepped forward, picking up one of the first pictures. "This is his wife, Apollinariya, and his son, Grigory, whom my grandfather is named for."

She set the picture down and continued. "Egor Alexeev, Nicholas's grandson, was well known throughout the St. Petersburg area and was one of the first doctors to specialize in the care of the Winter Palace's feline residents."

Dorothy suddenly turned away from the antique cattle medication dispenser and stared at Tatiana. "Did... Did Egor ever care for Kot'ka?"

Tatiana smiled mischievously. "You know your history, Ms. Fennec."

Dorothy shrugged. "I know some cat history."

"It's funny you mentioned Kot'ka. Egor performed his declaw due to Prince Alexei's affliction with hemophilia. Naturally, this put the Alexeev family in good standing with the tsars. Despite having no official titles or lands—though it is said my ancestors were offered many times but did not accept for political reasons—they were highly respected, and their counsel was at times requested even for some human ailments."

She took a few steps back, moving Dorothy down the line of heirlooms and pictures on the table. "During the Bolshevik Revolution in 1917, the Alexeevs turned from treating animals to treating the many orphaned children who congregated in children's camps."

She stopped and reached for the last picture. She stared, lost in memory, then held it out to Dorothy. It was the same picture of Alexei and Kot'ka Destin had shown during his briefing. "There is a rumor that Egor Alexeev was at Yekaterinburg the morning of July 16th, when the tsar and his family were executed. It's said he escaped with a few precious heirlooms, including Alexei's cat, who he took to the Winter Palace to live out its days."

Dorothy's grip on the end of her cane tightened. Her jaw clenched, trying to keep it from hanging open in awe. Tatiana did not understand what information she had just given her, but frankly, neither did Dorothy. Her mind raced through the family history again, landing on key points that she desperately tried to piece together. There was something there, something in that information, but she couldn't put her finger on it.

"Are you well, Ms. Fennec?" Tatiana asked, resting a hand on the old woman's arm.

Dorothy let out a breath, releasing her racing thoughts for another time. "Yes. I must have been daydreaming." She waved off the woman's concern. "Now, tell me more about your family."

Tatiana's worried face rose into excitement again. She guided Dorothy from the little room and through the conservatory to the gardens around the estate. She wove through paths lined with roses and other exotic plants. They circled around the property, entering this time through a side door that led to the lower levels of the kitchen and work areas. All the while, Dorothy hung on every word she spoke, which seemed to spur Tatiana on.

"In the early 1990s, after the fall of the USSR, many of the once abandoned and forgotten homes of the Russian aristocracy were reclaimed—or attempted to be reclaimed—by the original families. The infamous Golitsyn family once owned this house, but my grandfather purchased the property for, I think you Americans say pennies on the dollar, in 1993.

"That's when my mother moved in, as *Dedushka* was having a rough time getting around. I moved here with Maya after my divorce and threw myself into the history and renovations. I had hoped it would distract

Maya, but she and her *Praded* bonded immediately."

They stopped at the far end of the second-floor hall, pausing a moment to take in the crown moldings and gilded frames that lined the wallpapered walls.

"I'm very thankful for that bond," Tatiana mused. She turned away from the carved door frames, facing Dorothy and seeming torn whether to speak the thought hanging on the tip of her tongue.

"Mama!" came Maya's sudden and frantic voice from one of the rooms.

Tatiana dashed up the hall, Dorothy following in tow behind her. "Maya?" she called, wrenching one of the bedroom doors open.

The girl sat on the end of a tall four-poster bed, tears streaming down her face and her phone in one hand.

"What's wrong, love?" Tatiana rushed forward, sitting beside her daughter and taking the phone.

Maya buried her face in her hands, hot tears seeping through her fingers as Tatiana scrolled through the phone.

"That *svolach*," Tatiana whispered.

"He *is* a *svolach*!" Maya sobbed. "A stupid, stupid…" She hiccupped and took a deep breath. "*Praded* said everything happened for a reason. Everything happened so we could move here. But why did it happen like this?"

"What's wrong?" Dorothy asked. She hadn't liked the way Maya had reacted to Yury downstairs, and her thoughts turned to something sinister.

"I wish *Praded* was here." She leaned into her mother's arms, her cries coming in short, rattling breaths.

"I know, my love. Can I take Ms. Fennec downstairs? Then I'll be right back up. Okay?"

Maya hugged her mother tightly but finally released her. Tatiana rose, tucking the phone into her pocket and shutting the door to the bedroom behind her.

"Is she okay?" Dorothy asked.

Tatiana's gentle demeanor turned fierce and icy as soon as the door latched behind her. "It's her father. My ex," she said, shaking her head and holding back tears of her own. "When we moved here a few years ago, I told Maya it was to help my mother with *Praded*, but in truth, it's because I was fighting with Vlad over custody. She wants to spend time with her father, but he wants nothing to do with her. I told her he's very busy. It's the same lie I've been telling her for years. I think it's why she latched on to her *praded* so much, and why he gave her so many gifts, despite Yury's disapproval. But I suppose that cat's out of the bag now. Damnit… she couldn't have picked a worse time to find this out."

"Find what out?" Dorothy asked, her tone returning to the casual air she used when trying to wrest information from unsuspecting targets during her missions.

Reluctantly, Tatiana pulled the cell phone from her pocket. She hesitated but eventually unlocked the screen and handed it to Dorothy, holding her head in her hand.

A middle-aged man stood on the end of a boat, one arm wrapped around a young girl Dorothy thought might be his daughter. She flipped through the social media app to the next picture and gasped. The man was kissing the girl, and to Dorothy's surprise, not in a fatherly way.

"The *mudák* is having a glorious time in Bora Bora with a girl who used to be Maya's friend when they were little. I've been trying to keep it from her. She's a gentle girl and losing her great-grandfather has been a terrible strain on her. But now she's found out, and I—"

A high-pitched yowl filled the house. Tatiana and Dorothy took off running, the sound of a door opening and footsteps following close behind. They skidded to a halt in the entrance hall as Yury rounded the corner of the stairs. Solomon wiggled and cried as the man held tightly to his scruff, his other hand gripping Sandi's arm.

"Yury!" Tatiana cried. She rushed forward, Dorothy on her heels. "What are you doing?" She pulled the screaming cat from her uncle's grasp, easing Solomon safely back into Dorothy's arms as Maya stood on the top stair, her mouth open in horror.

"I want them out of here, Tatiana," he said, pushing Sandi unceremoniously at Dorothy. Sandi stumbled, but Tatiana steadied him. "I don't know why they're here, but they aren't welcome."

"Is that so?" Tatiana said, her hands flying to her hips.

"Yes, it's so. I found this one snooping around the house, and the damn cat was walking through the halls upstairs as if it owned the place."

"He... He knows how to open doors," Dorothy apologized, trying to console the cat that shook in her arms.

"Tell them I got lost finding the bathroom," Sandi whispered, rubbing the spot on his arm that Yury had grabbed.

Dorothy translated, and Tatiana turned back to her uncle, her eyebrows raised.

"The funeral is over. I expect them gone tomorrow." With that, Yury stormed up the stairs, pushing past Maya, who leapt out of his way and joined her mother at the bottom of the stairs.

"I am so, so sorry," Tatiana apologized, letting out a breath. "He hasn't always been like this." She reached out a hand to stroke Solomon, and the little cat lifted his head, pushing his nose into her palm.

"Death can make people behave in strange ways," Dorothy reassured her.

"He's been like this ever since *Praded* talked to him months ago," Maya said through her stuffy nose.

Tatiana shook her head. "He was skeptical of bringing guests and tourists into the house, but Grigory insisted that we needed to stay in St. Petersburg, and this was how we could afford to do so."

"Was Grigory opposed to moving?" Dorothy asked, shifting Solomon's position in her arms, though the little cat still clung to her with seemingly no intention of going anywhere.

"He used to live in a small apartment. With his health declining, it was either find a house that my mother could live in with him or move him to a nursing home. None of us wanted that, so he used his savings to purchase this place. It was an odd decision, but if we play it right, it could set our family up well for years."

"And Yury was against this?"

"Not at first, no. Skeptical, but Yury's always been skeptical of anything that wasn't his idea. And since it was what my grandfather wanted…" Tatiana shrugged. "He had a hand in controlling the finances for renovations. We didn't mind. He's always had a good mind for such things. But he suddenly changed his tune. He kept saying we didn't need to worry about guests and tourists. He said we'd be taken care of financially soon enough, but he wouldn't elaborate."

"*Djadja* said he found another way to afford the house," Maya said, and Tatiana patted her back. Dorothy watched as the girl waited to catch her mother's eye. When Tatiana continued on instead, she stared at the floor between her feet.

"Oh, listen to me! I shouldn't be telling you all this! I guess I've gotten so caught up in telling you the family's history. Please, forget I said anything." Tatiana waved a dismissive hand before her.

Dorothy gave her a comforting smile. "Don't worry about it. We'll be leaving as soon as we can arrange a flight back home."

Tatiana nodded and led Maya toward the dining room. Dorothy and Sandi watched them until they disappeared around the corner. Without a word, the two boarded the elevator, silent until it began to move.

"Did you find anything?" Dorothy asked.

Sandi shook his head. "Nothing. You?"

Something prickled at the back of Dorothy's mind,

wondering what Maya knew, what she wasn't saying and yet seemed so desperate to confide. Solomon chirped and trilled on her shoulder, suddenly realizing they were in an echoing chamber.

"I don't know. Tatiana's tour revealed what I think is some very important information. I have no idea how to piece it together, but I'm worried we're out of time."

"Do you think the girl knows anything?"

"I think she has a unique insight, but to what, I don't know."

"She seems to believe Yury has some kind of plan to make money. Could it be connected to the artifact?"

Dorothy shushed Solomon as he meowed louder, trying to make the sound echo in the elevator. "She's also going through quite an emotional ordeal right now. She was very close to Grigory, and she's just found out her father's been lying to her. I think the girl is more distraught than anything." Dorothy wasn't sure she entirely believed what she said, but there wasn't the time to investigate every lead.

The elevator began to slow, and they felt the tiny bump as it stopped on the third floor.

"Then I suppose we'll be visiting the basement tonight," Sandi said before stepping out into the hall.

NINE

MAINTAINING AN ACTIVE LIFESTYLE MEANT Dorothy had yet to succumb to many of the rigors that age brought with it. Muscle atrophy, diseases like adult diabetes or kidney disease were almost commonplace among her childhood friends. But good genes and a stubborn persistence to live long enough to see the entire world had kept these ailments at bay. Sleep, on the other hand, was an entirely different matter.

Dorothy and Sandi retired to their rooms after the incident with Yury. Though Tatiana insisted otherwise, Dorothy felt it would be best to stay out from under the man's suspicious eye. The staff brought them dinner in their rooms, and they turned in early after discussing a new plan.

She had easily slept for six hours, which, twenty years ago, would have been enough. But now that she was creeping closer to seventy, it took every ounce of willpower in her to unwrap herself from Solomon's cuddles and climb from beneath the covers to dress. Solomon yawned and stretched, the little toes of his back feet splaying outward before he decided it was far too cold and burrowing beneath Dorothy's abandoned covers.

Wishing she hadn't eaten so heavy before sleeping, Dorothy removed her nightgown, dressing in some of the athletic wear she had recently purchased now that she was working out more regularly. She pulled her silver hair back, tying it into a quick braid. She ran her fingers along the beautiful hair stick Red had given her. It was like having him with her, but if something happened, she didn't want to risk losing it. She laid it softly on the dresser, her fingers lingering over its ornate surface for a moment longer.

Solomon's head suddenly poked from beneath the blankets, and moments later, Dorothy heard Sandi knock quietly on the washroom door. She opened it, though this time, Solomon chose to chirp at the man from his cozy blanket den instead of accosting his ankles.

"nǐ zhǔn bèi hǎo chū fā le?" Sandi asked.

Dorothy tapped her ear, then retrieved the Babel ear cuff from her side table. She clipped it on and was greeted by the seashell-like sound once more.

"Are you ready?" Sandi asked, and this time, Dorothy heard his words translated.

"Almost," she said, pulling Solomon's carrier from beneath the bed. She unzipped the top, clicking her tongue to get the cat's attention. He poked his head out again, blinking and yawning widely. When he appeared as if he had no intention of moving, Dorothy scooped him from beneath the covers, and secured his harness around him. With a kiss on his head, she placed him inside, zipped the top, and slung the bag over her shoulder. He was less likely to make noise while in the carrier, or she hoped anyway.

Sandi bowed to her and adjusted what looked like a fanny pack around his waist. They heard the clock strike three from the library, sending a chilling reverberation throughout the house. That was their cue.

They crept down the servant's stairwell Tatiana had shown her earlier that day. They stopped at the second-floor entrance, listening intently. Silence greeted them, and the occasional snore from somewhere in the distance. Each step they took creaked, no matter how slow or careful they stepped. But slow and careful they were. When they finally reached the first floor, they slid open the pocket door to the kitchen, listening for several long moments. Still nothing. Through the dining room and into the entrance hall they moved, past the murals whose painted eyes followed Dorothy's every move. But there was only silence. Silence and the ominous settling of an old house in the night.

"Ready?" Sandi asked, pulling aside the gate for the elevator he had sent down to the first floor before coming for Dorothy.

Dorothy took a deep, controlled breath, adjusting the carrier on her shoulder and playing with the grip on her cane. "Ready."

Solomon mewed as well, and Dorothy's breath hitched. Sandi quickly closed the door, throwing them into complete darkness.

"He's restless," Dorothy whispered. "We need to hurry."

She couldn't see, but Sandi must have heard her. He pulled out his phone and, using the artificial glow, pressed the button for the basement just as Solomon began chirping.

"Hush!" Dorothy quipped, more loudly than she had spoken for some time.

Solomon quieted his meows until the elevator bumped to a halt. They stared at the closed door before them, its peeling white paint sending something of a silent warning for what lay beyond. They each produced a small flashlight as Sandi pulled back the gate and opened the door.

The room smelled of must and earth and was completely dark. Their flashlights roamed over stacks of wooden crates, pieces of furniture covered in plastic, and other various items one would expect. There was, however, no obvious sign of a vault—keypad, door or otherwise.

"See if you can find a light source," Sandi said.

Dorothy adjusted Solomon's carrier on her shoulder and headed left as Sandi headed right. Her light passed back and forth between the wall and the path before her. Her skin crawled as she thought of the spiders and rats that were most certainly taking refuge in the space. She reached the corner and turned, a tiny yelp escaping her lips as her light passed over the Neoclassical style statue of a man.

With her heart still pounding, she continued. A loud snap echoed throughout the space. Solomon gave a tiny hiss inside the carrier as an electrical buzz sounded above them, and antique lights flickered to life.

Dorothy's mouth fell open. Three rounded doorways led to other rooms filled with heirlooms and treasures. And, if she was to believe what her flashlight revealed, each of those rooms led to at least one more. She clicked off her flashlight, shoving it into one of the pockets of Solomon's carrier.

"Maybe there isn't a vault," she said. "What if this *is* the vault?"

"We'll never search all these boxes and crates in time," said Sandi, winding his way past a stack of wooden boxes taller than he was to join her.

Dorothy crossed her arms, her eyes still taking in the contents of the room. "There has to be an order to this. We just can't see it." She stepped toward one of the pieces of furniture covered in a sheet of plastic. She lifted it and ran her hand over the cushion. "Yes, this was only recently moved down here. See? No dust."

She stepped through the closest doorway. The room was filled with construction equipment, likely used as a work room for the renovators. The room beyond it was full of plastic shelves and boxes of modern construction material.

Sandi followed quietly as Dorothy worked, moving boxes out of the way or holding Solomon's carrier as she investigated the accumulated heirlooms. They entered the final room, this one illuminated with only a single light. They pulled out their flashlights again and noticed many of the boxes had been cleared to the sides as opposed to stacked haphazardly with no rhyme or reason.

"Now that's odd," he declared.

Dorothy didn't answer. There was a definite

temperature difference in the center of the room. She held her hand out, taking a step backward and forward. Old homes were known to have cold spots. A few years ago, she would have dismissed tales of ghosts as the culprit. But this wasn't a cold spot—ghost or otherwise. It was far too large of an area. She walked farther into it, her hand held out before her, trying to feel where the temperature grew warm again.

Finally, her hand rested against the back wall. It was like ice. She moved to the corner and touched the side wall a few feet in. Even within the mass of cold, it was several degrees warmer.

"Sandi?" Dorothy asked tentatively. "Where are we in relation to the above floors?"

Sandi handed Solomon's carrier back to her, heading toward the elevator where she heard him counting as he stepped. As he rounded the corner, he stopped, a grin spreading across his face.

"Why, I do believe we are behind the alcoves in the entrance hall."

"The ones with the mysterious empty spaces behind them?" Dorothy's own smile widened. She took a step back, taking in the room as a whole. "Most of this basement is not original to the house, save for that first part. It looks like it was built in the late 1800s."

"Or early 1900s," said Sandi. "Around the time of

the first World War, perhaps?"

Dorothy closed her eyes, hoping her memory was still sharp. She stood there silent, her mind thinking back to her tour with Tatiana, back to her tour at St. Isaac's Cathedral. *Always at the front, my love.*

Dorothy's eyes shot open. "It's a tunnel."

"What?"

Dorothy shook her head. She had to calm the myriad of thoughts, put them in the proper order, but her heart raced with excitement. "The Winter Palace was originally just a small wooden building. But, in 1730, Anna Ivanovna commissioned a grand stone palace be built after Dmitry Golitsyn helped put her on the throne. After it was built, she had him sentenced to death." She turned to look at Sandi, her eyes wide with excitement. "Grigory's ancestor took Kot'ka to safety to the Winter Palace to live out his days, and Grigory himself bought this place in the 1990s. Tatiana said this house was originally owned by the Golitsyn family."

"Are you saying the artifact isn't here?" Sandi asked.

"Exactly," Dorothy said, turning back to the wall and running her hands over the cold brick. "It's in the Winter Palace, and Grigory knew that. If he promised the artifact to Destin but didn't have it in his possession, that could be why the will was changed."

A brick moved several inches at Dorothy's touch.

She kept pushing, wiggling it until she could get her fingers over the edge. She pulled it free and lifted her flashlight into the tiny space. An old iron door hinge shone back at her out of the darkness.

"The Golitsyns always had a hand in Russian political affairs. Of course they would have a secret entrance into, or rather, out of, the Winter Palace. Grigory must have known this, which is why he bought this house over thirty years ago."

She handed brick after brick to Sandi until she had revealed the handle to the door and a hole large enough for them to climb through. She rested her hand on the cold metal of the doorknob.

"Thank you, my love," she whispered, and turned the handle.

The excitement that had been building within her immediately deflated. Of course it was locked. Why wouldn't it be? She rattled it again, hoping that perhaps it was just stuck. She felt a hand on her shoulder and jumped.

"Let me," Sandi whispered.

She stepped aside and watched as he pulled a thin, leather-bound case from his pack.

"How..." Dorothy began, but realized if he packed his fanny pack with the same efficiency he had packed his suitcase, then there could be an entire laptop in there, and she'd never know it.

Sandi unrolled the case, revealing an old lock picking kit. "Not all systems require code and computers," he said.

Solomon wiggled and mewed in protest in the carrier as Sandi worked. Dorothy could hear the desperation in the little cat's tone. He was so tired of being cooped up, and she couldn't blame him. She tried to console him as she held the flashlight for Sandi, whispering words of encouragement that the Babel artifact had no hope of translating for her.

Finally, the tumblers seemed to move. Sandi put away his kit and tested the handle. It took both hands, but it did eventually turn with an echoing creak that reverberated all around them. They stood still, waiting for the sound to die away. Sandi leaned through the hole, pushing the door as wide as he could, where a blast of cold air met them. It did not smell like the earthy basement they were in, but rather, filtered and recycled.

"Air conditioning?" he asked.

"If it's from the Winter Palace or the Hermitage Museum now, then yes."

Sandi bowed. "Shall we?" He put away his kit and climbed through the hole with ease. Once situated on the other side, he pulled out his flashlight again, shining it down the dark tunnel.

"Can you see anything?" Dorothy asked.

The light revealed high stone walls and brick flooring. There was no electricity, at least none that they could see. No light bulbs hanging from the wooden rafters of the ceiling or even oil lamps hung on the walls. There was nothing.

They heard the clock chime four o'clock in the library above them, and Dorothy's heart quickened. Surely the staff would be awake soon to prepare breakfast and begin their daily chores. She joined Sandi through the hole in the wall, cursing herself for not making it larger. When she had dusted off her clothes and pulled out her own flashlight, they began their trek down the dark tunnel.

The pair walked in silence, their footsteps surprisingly quiet against the ancient brick. Solomon wiggled in his carrier, and the two took turns managing his weight over their shoulders. Dorothy stared at her watch every few minutes, her pace quickening into almost a jog after a half hour. Sandi kept pace for a short bit, but it wasn't until her knee began to throb from the exertion that she slowed again.

"I'm going to have to talk to Dr. Jon about these injections," she said, leaning into the cane.

Sandi stopped abruptly beside her, and Dorothy

halted her pace. A few feet before them stood another door, identical to the first.

"Please tell me you know how to shut off the security cameras once we get in there," Dorothy whispered.

She couldn't see his face, but the Babel artifact gave a peculiar inflection to his tone. "If I don't, I suppose this will be our last mission then."

She assumed he meant the retort in jest, but her paranoia over the whole situation being a setup from Destin made the hair on her arms stand on end.

Sandi pulled out his lock pick kit again and got to work, this time more quickly, as he was now familiar with the style of tumbler. Dorothy held the flashlight aloft, shushing Solomon as he had begun his chirping and mewing once more. The tumblers moved into place, and Solomon gave a pitiful, whining meow.

"Solomon!" Dorothy scolded, louder than she had intended.

They waited, silent and still as the echo of her voice slowly faded. Then they heard movement. Even Solomon stopped his pacing in the carrier. Dorothy flicked off her flashlight, but it wasn't fast enough. The doorknob rattled, and they retreated to the corners at either side of the door, shrouding themselves in darkness.

The doorknob continued to twist and turn as

whoever was on the other side tried to open it. But as quickly as it had started, it stopped. Dorothy held her breath as she watched light pass beneath the edge of the door, revealing a shadow that slowly moved away. She counted to sixty, then flicked on her flashlight, shining it at her face. She gestured toward the estate side of the tunnel, and Sandi nodded his head. She turned the light off and picked Solomon's carrier off the floor behind her. As Dorothy passed before the door, the little cat gave a long, low growl.

With a resounding crash, the door was kicked open, sending bits of wood splintering toward Dorothy. She crouched, shielding herself and Solomon from both the shards of wood and the blinding light that shone behind the figure.

"Well, it appears we've both hit a dead end."

Dorothy whipped around, forcing her eyes to adjust to the person standing before them.

"Mary Ann?"

TEN

THE WOMAN ADJUSTED THE GUN HOLSTER SLUNG over her shoulder and patted an obviously unpregnant belly.

"It's so easy to smuggle anything onto a plane if you play up the flustered pregnant woman trope. They won't even do a search if you cry hard enough. But if you're all the way down here, then that must mean the egg wasn't in Grigory's house after all."

"Hello?" a distant voice called. "Who's there?"

"Oh, now that's a shame. I liked her." Mary Ann removed one of the guns at her side and stepped through the door.

Without thinking, Dorothy held out her cane at the last moment. Mary Ann stumbled but did not fall. Instead, she turned, a wry smile spreading across her face.

"I assure you, we may be on opposing sides, but we both want the same thing. I advise you not to get in my way," Mary Ann warned.

"Hello?" said the voice again, this time much closer, and Dorothy thought she saw a tiny point of light in the distance. "Is everything all right down here?"

Dorothy's heart skipped a beat. It was Tatiana.

"You leave her out of this," Dorothy seethed.

Mary Ann laughed. "She inserted herself, I'm afraid. Curiosity and cats and all."

"No, Mary Ann," said Sandi. "We can't afford such a risk when we don't even have the artifact."

Dorothy's mouth fell open, but there was no time for her to comprehend how Sandi knew Mary Ann's name.

"Ms. Fennec?" came Tatiana's voice.

"Tatiana! Don't come any closer! Get out of here!" Dorothy screamed.

"We have no idea what conclusions she'll draw!" Mary Ann snapped at Sandi, who shrank into the corner. She raised her gun and pointed her flashlight up the tunnel.

The light at the far end of the tunnel stopped when Mary Ann's cry echoed off the stone walls.

"Fennec!" Sandi shrieked as Dorothy lifted her cane again to strike at Mary Ann.

But the woman was younger, faster. She grabbed the end of the cane, attempting to pull it from Dorothy's grasp. Dorothy felt it give just beneath the silver embellishment. She pulled in return, and Mary Ann fell flat on her back as the hidden sword within pulled free.

Tatiana's light was coming closer again. Dorothy backed away from Mary Ann and Sandi as Solomon clawed at the zipper of the carrier, yowling in desperation to be set free. Dorothy heard Tatiana gasp as she drew within a few yards of the scene.

"Tatiana! I said get back!" Dorothy cried again, trying to position herself between Tatiana and Mary Ann.

With a final push against her side, Solomon freed himself through the opening in the zipper he had created. He circled around, coming to stand between Dorothy's feet, his hackles raised, and his eyes dilated, even in the bright artificial light of the flashlights, and the museum room beyond.

Mary Ann aimed her gun again, this time lowering the barrel away from Tatiana and toward the little black cat.

Dorothy didn't believe much in ghosts, but she did believe in luck. Instinct, intuition, and sheer dumb luck. At the last moment, she turned the sword in her hand, thrusting it into the ground in front of Solomon.

The sound of gunfire filled the stone tunnel, and she felt the bullet ricochet off the blade. Solomon slunk back into the darkness as Dorothy stood straight again. Mary Ann's mouth fell open and Sandi slipped away through the darkness of the still-open door.

"Tatiana, take Solomon and get out of here," said Dorothy. "No matter what he does, get him out."

Behind her, Dorothy heard Solomon's wild protests, but Tatiana's trained hands restrained him, and she took off into the darkness back to the estate.

Mary Ann got to her feet, slipping the gun back into her holster. "That was impressive, I must confess."

"You tried to kill my cat."

"Look, I'm no art historian, but I've got the brawn to get us through whatever traps have been set around this thing."

"You tried to *kill* my cat."

Mary Ann held her hands up. "If we just work together, we can figure out who has jurisdiction over the damn egg once we find it."

"You tried to *kill* my *cat*!" With muscle memory she long since thought was forgotten after her jiu-jitsu tournaments had ended decades ago, Dorothy raised the blade in a single motion, the tip poised inches before Mary Ann's throat.

More lights came to life in the room beyond the

door, and Dorothy could hear boots and deliberate movement within. A smile spread across Mary Ann's face as she carefully pulled a piece of shiny fabric from inside her sleeve cuff.

"So sorry, Fennec. I quite like you."

In an instant, she vanished, leaving Dorothy still poised with the sword pointed in the air as the Russian Federal Security Service stepped through the door.

&LEVEN

THREE RUSSIAN POLICE OFFICERS LED DOROTHY
down the front steps of the Hermitage Museum
with her hands cuffed behind her back. They took
everything from her. Solomon's carrier, her phone,
the cane, which had been reassembled into one
piece again. They even took the Babel ear cuff.

There weren't many people awake yet, but a handful
of onlookers crowded behind the erected barriers as
the police ran their investigation. Dorothy heard them
speaking but could no longer understand them. It was
a stark reminder that she was in bigger trouble than
she had ever been before.

She was an American visiting Russia under strange
circumstances. If she contacted the U.S. Embassy,
she might get released from Russia but still charged
for conspiracy back in the States. She hadn't exactly

entered the country in the most legal way. Fanny Fennec may have been her alias, but it was not a legal name. Working for a secret organization had unique advantages, but there were still more than enough cons to outweigh the pros. She walked in silence, flanked by several large, armed officers, her mind working overtime on a plan of escape.

As her escort marched her down the plain white corridor at the police station, past thick metal doors and bright florescent lights, her only hope was Solomon was safe. If she never made it out of here, Tatiana would take care of him. They led her into a small room. A single wooden chair sat beside a desk whose varnish had started to peel away decades ago. The wallpaper was something straight out of the fifties, and the only light above the desk flickered ominously. One officer removed her handcuffs and set them on the table in front of her, a clear reminder of who was still in control. He dismissed all but one of the other men, who closed the door behind them with a loud thud.

"*Ya stolknulsya s nekotorymi interesnymi situatsiyami zdes', v Sankt-Peterburge, no eta stala ochen' vysokoy v moyem spiske,*" said the first officer. He removed his hat, smoothing his honey colored hair and crossing his arms.

Dorothy cleared her throat. "I'm sorry. I don't speak Russian. Can you provide me an interpreter?" It was the same line she had been repeating since they'd taken her ear cuff.

The two officers shared a glance, wry smiles pulling at their lips, and making Dorothy swallow nervously again.

"But you were speaking Russian so well at the Hermitage," the second officer chided, switching now to heavily accented English.

"*Glupyy amerikanets. Oni tak legko zabyvayut, net?*"

Dorothy ignored the roaring laughter that followed whatever the first officer had said. "The officers on scene must have made a mistake. I'm an American. I cannot speak or understand Russian."

"Are you saying Denis is a liar?" the first asked.

Dorothy rubbed her knees and legs nervously. She had only ever heard of this tactic in movies or books, but it seemed like she was being backed into a corner, forced to admit to something she hadn't done, and her lack of sleep wasn't helping matters.

"Absolutely not. But it doesn't change the fact that I don't speak Russian, so I do very much appreciate you accommodating me now."

The officers crossed their arms almost in unison, towering over Dorothy.

"All right, we'll do it your way then," the first said, opening a folder of papers already on the table before their arrival. "You told Denis you were here with a… Mr. Sandi. Who is Mr. Sandi?"

"He's my friend," Dorothy replied, relaxing only slightly.

"What kind of friend? One does not travel halfway around the world for just anyone." He raised an eyebrow at her.

"It's not like that. I'm in a relationship, thank you," she said, raising her own eyebrow and hoping the gesture wasn't too out of line.

"And your lover approves of you traveling with another man?"

"He's well aware."

The first officer nodded, seeming flummoxed with being unable to catch Dorothy as some kind of runaway wife. "So, you traveled to Russia with your *friend*. Why?"

"He wanted to pay his respects to Grigory Alexeev."

"Did he say why?" the second officer asked.

"Sandi's father and Grigory served in the war together."

"Hmm." The first rubbed his chin and began pacing behind the desk. "Intriguing. So, how did you get into the Hermitage at 4:30 in the morning if you were there to pay your respects to Grigory Nikitovich Alexeev?"

"It was a mistake," Dorothy said, trying not to

hesitate, though she worried she may have spoken too quickly. She rubbed her knees again, both from nerves and the pain that throbbed in them.

"I see. Do you make it a habit of breaking into historical sites and brandishing swords at ghosts?"

"I told you it was a mistake."

"And were you hoping to hide some stolen art in your animal carrier or was that for the ghost too?" the second asked.

They were wearing her down. Dorothy could feel it. Wearing her down and pushing her to her limits. For the first time in a long time, Dorothy just wanted someone with her. She didn't need saving or for someone to fight her battle for her. She wanted comfort, the calming presence of Red or Aaron. Even the shudder-some postman, Mr. Altman, was better than being alone.

"I'd like to make a phone call, please," she said, hoping it would at least stall for time.

The two officers burst out laughing again.

"*Amerikanets khochet yey odin telefonnyy zvonok, Stas,*" the first officer said, clapping his partner on the shoulder.

"*O, davay dadim eto yey. Eto mozhet byt' zabavno.*"

The first officer nodded and reached under the desk, pulling out an old corded phone.

"*Prodolzhat'*. Call whoever you like," he said, then almost snorted with delight.

Dorothy stared at the phone on the table. She had no idea who to call. Aaron certainly couldn't help her, and if by some miracle she *did* get out of this mess, she didn't want to worry him. Destin had already said there was no way to get her out. Not for the first time, she wondered if Mary Ann, Sandi, everything had all been a setup to quietly get rid of her in a foreign country.

Her hand rubbed against the side of her leg as her nerves started to get the better of her. It wasn't until she felt the outline of a business card in her pocket that her hands stopped shaking. She didn't remember putting it there, but perhaps it was simply habit now. She pulled it out and reached for the receiver.

It was several hours since Dorothy set the receiver back on its base with trembling fingers. The sun that had started to rise when she'd left the Hermitage was now overcast with a blanket of gray clouds. Outside, the bustle of the city had picked up, and the only thing that hinted at the passage of time was the fervent blaring of car horns in the streets below.

On one hand, Dorothy was glad the officers had left

her alone. They were more than happy to do so after what had taken place on the other end of the phone. On the other, she was sure the stress of waiting for an unknown outcome was taking years off her life.

Dorothy had dialed the number on the business card and listened as the phone rang repeatedly. She had almost given up when the line clicked, and silence replaced the ringing.

"Hello?" she had said tentatively, trying to keep from glancing at the officers who towered over her.

Silence. Then a series of clicks.

"This is Dorothy Cl—Fennec."

More clicks greeted her, then a woman's voice came on the line, barely audible through a cloud of static. "Password."

Dorothy sat in silence as the static on the other end of the phone crackled and popped. Finally, she spoke the only thing that came to her mind. "*Materia Prima*."

There were another series of clicks, and the line went silent again. Worried she had said something wrong, Dorothy started to pull the receiver away from her ear when the static suddenly cleared, and a familiar voice sounded on the other end.

"Hello, Dorothy. Thank you for calling."

"H-Hello, Robbie," she said, her voice strained. "I… I need help."

"It would seem that way, yes. Please, put one of the officers on the line for me."

Stunned, Dorothy handed the phone to the first officer, unsure how Robbie knew they were with her in the first place. The man took it, though the smile on his face suddenly vanished.

"*Allo*?" he said into the phone.

Dorothy couldn't hear Robbie's words, but the color in his face drained. He stuttered, not quite getting a full word out at a time. Then, he hung up the phone and left the room with the other officer in tow.

It wasn't long before she realized they weren't coming back. Her stomach began to grumble, and she'd tried to nap through a wave of nausea, her hunger pangs trying to get the better of her. For a while, she thought perhaps they would leave her in the room to starve. How long could she survive without food? Without water? Should she dare try opening the window and escape?

When a break in the clouds bathed the street below in a wash of sunshine, she crept to the window and studied the shadows on the ground. It must have been shortly before or after noon. She heard footsteps heading down the hall for what seemed like the hundredth time. So, when the door opened wide, it caught her off guard. She slunk away from the window as the first officer held the door for Robbie Hodge.

Robbie was exactly as Dorothy remembered from her first, and only, meeting with him. He smiled coyly when he saw her and motioned for the officers to leave. They did so with great haste, closing the door behind them. Robbie sat in the single chair and stretched out, cupping his hands behind his head as he made himself comfortable.

"Thank you for calling," he said.

Dorothy didn't reply. She still wasn't sure why she had done so, or why *Materia Prima* had been the correct password. *If* it was the password at all.

"How is Solomon?" he continued.

Dorothy's pent-up anger suddenly bubbled to the surface. It took every ounce of self-control not to unleash it on Robbie, who had done nothing but come to her aid. At least, she hoped that was why he had come.

"He's safe," she said.

Robbie nodded, his smile spreading. "See, this is why I like you. You don't say more than is needed. The mark of a good agent."

Dorothy scoffed, turning toward the window and staring out at the street below. "Some agent. I wasn't able to retrieve the artifact."

Robbie waved his hand in the air. "A minor setback. But I'm here to rectify that."

Dorothy's eyes fixated on Robbie, and the man raised his hands in defense.

"I'm not here to force you to take sides. I've already asked you once to leave the Foxes. I will not push. But I know that you know there's more to the Foxes than meets the eye."

"What do you know that I know? And how do I know it isn't a lie?"

Robbie laughed, leaning forward onto the desk between them. "Because I don't lie, unlike some people I know. Like you, I may not tell the whole truth at once, but I never lie. And I will prove it to you."

He removed a strange-looking watch on his wrist and flicked the light switch on the wall. Light still shone in from the window, but as Robbie twiddled with the watch, Dorothy saw a projection glimmer to life in the air.

"This is a replica of the night sky above us right now," he said, twiddling more knobs. The projection shifted, but only slightly. "This is what the night sky will look like in two days over the Hermitage Museum. But you know this already. You also know this is the constellation engraved on the egg that Destin sent you to retrieve."

Dorothy's face blanched, but she kept her emotions still.

"Now, here's what you don't know," Robbie went on. "Destin knows exactly what that egg will do when it aligns with this constellation in the sky, and it's why he wants it. Don't you find it odd that he has no connections here in Russia, but his reach extends to almost every other country?"

"The Foxes are a controversial organization," Dorothy said.

"Indeed. Controversial because they, and only they, get to decide which artifacts may remain loose in the world, which ones the agents may use, and which stay under Destin's lock and key. I, for one, don't find that a comforting thought. For this reason, I sent one of my own agents to retrieve the egg before Destin's team could swoop in. I set things up months in advance with Yury to change Grigory's will and keep Destin's prying hands out of one more Earth relic that he believes himself master of."

Out of the thousands of thoughts that fought for attention in Dorothy's mind, she landed on only one. "It was you, then! You and Mary Ann and Sandi! You almost killed Tatiana. You almost killed Solomon!"

Robbie hung his head. "I... I am terribly sorry for Mary Ann's actions. She didn't know. That's why I asked about him. Honest."

"Destin may have his own reasons for what he does,

but he doesn't go around *killing* innocent lives in the process!"

"Doesn't he?"

Dorothy opened her mouth to speak but closed it again. She unclenched her fists, though her jaw was locked tight. She knew exactly what Robbie meant, but she wasn't going to give him the satisfaction of asking about her father. No matter how much her heart screamed to. She took several deep breaths as he went on.

"Dorothy, I need help getting that egg, and I can't do it without you. I'm not asking you to pick sides, but I am asking you to return the favor. I'll help you get out of here, and you help me get that egg before it's too late."

Dorothy thought for several long moments. She turned back to the window, though her eyes remained unfocused. She knew Destin was lying to her. She'd known it for quite some time. And there were other agents who seemed to know as well. Dr. Jon. Sandi.

Sandi had switched sides, or at least that's how it appeared. How else would he have known Mary Ann, and why else would he have left Dorothy to face off against her in the tunnel? Then again, he might be working as a double agent. There simply wasn't enough information to know, and for that reason, Dorothy wasn't about to jump ship so quickly.

She faced Robbie, her anger replaced with a heightened awareness. "What does the egg do?"

Robbie sighed and shook his head. "Now, that wasn't our agreement, Ms. *Fennec*."

"It wasn't yours, but it's mine."

It was Robbie's turn to sit in silence as Dorothy stared him down. He switched off the projection on his watch and placed it back on his wrist.

"The Constellation Egg is a catalyst. It holds a power that would tip the balance of control throughout the world. It would start like a ripple and slowly move to all four corners of the world. Whoever holds that power controls that balance. Satisfied?"

"Not entirely," Dorothy quipped.

"Good. You should never be fully satisfied, but that's all I'm giving you. Now, we can walk out of here together, or I can let the officers in the hall back in. I won't consider you coming with me a sign of permanent allegiance, but you would be wise to do so. I don't think I need to list all the reasons why."

He held out a hand to her, waiting for Dorothy to accept his offer. She looked at the back of the closed door, then shook Robbie's hand.

TWELVE

ROBBIE ABRUPTLY LEFT THE ROOM, LEAVING Dorothy standing with her hand still in the air. As the door closed behind him, she pulled back the sleeve of her blouse, checking her hand and wrist for any signs of… well, she wasn't sure. If her time with the Foxes had taught her anything, it was that anything could be an artifact. But her fears subsided when he returned moments later, the door held wide and the officers standing perplexed in the hall behind him.

"It's all taken care of," he said. He held out her cane, and a plastic bag with the rest of her possessions. She took the cane and pulled the Babel artifact from the bag. She never felt so relieved for muffled hearing. Once outside, she checked her phone, but it was clearly dead. Not that she had any clue who to call. She stared at the busy street before her as Robbie pulled out his own cell phone.

"Hello, may I speak with Tatiana Denisovna?" he asked in Russian. He stood in silence, ignoring Dorothy's lingering presence. "Ah, hello madam. This is Mr. Hodge. Yes, that Hodge. Yes. I need you to bring a car to the district police station on Nevsky. Ms. Fennec is waiting. Yes, she's well. Completely released and cleared of all charges. Ah, I'll let her explain that. And, please have lunch ready for her as well. Thank you."

Robbie ended the call as Dorothy's stomach gave another gurgle. He smiled coyly, and she looked away, unsure of anything anymore.

"Thank you," she mustered.

"Of course. You've been in there for hours. You could use a hot meal and rest before venturing into the Hermitage again."

Dorothy shook her head. "So, you knew everything? You knew I was on this mission? You knew the artifact was in the Hermitage? You even knew Sandi was with me, and yet you left me to gallivant around like an idiot?"

"As much as I like you, Dorothy, I'm afraid you still work for Destin Hollanday at the moment, and that is more dangerous to me than needlessly blowing the cover of my own agents."

"So, you admit that Sandi works for you."

"I don't make it a habit to reveal the secrets of others without their permission. Good day, my lady. I'm sure we'll see each other soon."

With that, Robbie walked across the busy street, his pace set perfectly to avoid the onslaught of traffic that passed by. Dorothy watched him go until a van drove past her vision, and Robbie Hodge seemed to blink out of sight.

A shiver ran up Dorothy's spine. It might have been the wind that whipped around her, but she was sure it was more likely that she had witnessed an artifact in use. So much of their conversation dominated her thoughts as she stood waiting on the sidewalk outside the police station. Thoughts she was no longer sure were her own, but suggestions planted by all the people she had met in the last year and a half.

A black car pulled up to the curb, and Dorothy didn't notice until it had parked in front of her. She snapped herself out of the daze she had slipped into and approached the vehicle. The rear door opened, and a stern-faced Tatiana stared up at her. The two woman locked eyes for a moment, then Tatiana moved over, allowing Dorothy to climb in. They rode in silence back to Grigory's estate, and it wasn't until the car had pulled away from the front steps did Tatiana speak.

"Solomon is all right."

It was the last thing Dorothy expected to hear, but the one thing she needed. She let out a shuddering sob, thankful for the cane that held her on her feet. She buried her face in her free hand, letting every emotion she hadn't realized she had been holding in flow out of her. She saw Tatiana take a tentative step forward through her blurry vision and felt the woman's hand on her shoulder.

"It wasn't supposed to be like this," Dorothy whispered through ragged breaths. "It's all gotten out of hand."

She felt Tatiana's grip on her shoulder tighten in comfort, and somewhere, she produced a handkerchief, setting it in Dorothy's hand. Dorothy took several deep breaths and wiped the tears from her face. When she looked at Tatiana, she saw the woman's own eyes glassy with tears.

"I must be honest with you, Ms. Fennec. Everything about this situation tells me to run away, but there's something about you I can't put my finger on. Something that's not as it appears."

"None of this is as it appears," Dorothy said, her sobs finally controlled.

"I need to know what happened down there," Tatiana answered, her voice more stern. "If my family is in danger, I must know. Mr. Sandi won't tell me anything. He's locked himself in his room, and the only reason I haven't kicked him out is because I don't want Yury to know. I'd never live it down."

"Tatiana, I can't. It's too dangerous."

Tatiana pressed her lips into a thin line. She flipped her long hair behind her, tapping her foot as she thought. She sighed as Dorothy handed the handkerchief back, her lips rising into a compassionate smile. "Well, if I'm going to be a hostess, I might as well play the part. Come, Mr. Hodge said to serve you lunch, and lunch you shall be served. Besides, I know a little black cat who misses his human terribly."

To Dorothy's surprise, Tatiana took her free arm, leading her up the steps and through the front doors. The house was quiet. More so than yesterday during Grigory's funeral. She assumed most of the family had left, though the quiet unsettled her. No wonder Tatiana felt the need to fill the house with talk and laughter. Tatiana opened the door to the elevator, and Dorothy stopped, her memory flooded with the sound of gunfire from the night before.

"Ms. Fennec?" Tatiana said.

Dorothy shook her head and entered the elevator. She stood quiet, occasionally wiping a rogue tear from her cheek. The elevator glided past the second floor and settled gently on the third. Before Tatiana opened the door, Dorothy heard the mournful and desperate mews of Solomon, and her heart leapt with joy.

The door opened, and Dorothy fell back against the wall as a ball of fur launched itself into her arms. Solomon rubbed his face all over hers, wiping away any tears that remained on her cheeks. She lowered herself to the floor, burying her face in the little cat's coat, and letting the sound of his purring envelope her.

Tatiana stood patiently outside the elevator door, letting human and cat have their moment. When Solomon was thoroughly satisfied, he stepped from Dorothy's lap, and sat at Tatiana's feet, waiting for Dorothy to follow.

Dorothy's knees cracked as she pushed herself to her feet and followed both cat and vet to her room. To her surprise, what few decorations had been in the room were removed or lying on the floor. The bed appeared as if it had been made up at one time, but someone had dug at the pillows and sheets, and possibly burrowed beneath the comforter. Solomon's food dish was completely upended, and food bits were scattered from the door all the way to the bathroom.

Tatiana hung her head. "He's been protesting," she said. "I'll have someone come clean this when I bring your food."

"No, I'll clean it. I'm sorry for the trouble he's

caused. The trouble I've caused." Dorothy pulled out her suitcase unpacking a smaller bag within that held Solomon's travel supplies. She produced a can of food and a small brush and dustpan.

"Perhaps you can tell me about this trouble when I come back."

Dorothy paused, the hair on her arms and neck standing on end. She didn't know who she could trust anymore. She had never been above asking for help on missions when she needed it. Karlee. Hulda. But something was different now. Something had changed within her.

"I can't drag you into this, Tatiana," she said, standing to look the woman in the eye.

"But you already have."

Tatiana shut the door behind her, and Solomon immediately pounced at the handle, his bent little tail wagging back and forth in excitement.

Dorothy finished cleaning up the wayward kibble and tucked the brush and dustpan back in her bag. Tatiana was right. She was already involved. She knew about the tunnel. She knew Dorothy had been in an altercation with someone—someone that had tried to kill her. It was difficult to know what she had seen and heard in the dim light and echoing space. She was right that her family might be in danger. The question was how much more risk was Dorothy willing to take on this mission.

There was a gentle knock on the bathroom door, and Solomon bolted toward it, shoving his paws beneath the gap and playfully swiping at whoever was on the other side. Dorothy nudged the little cat aside and opened the door. Sandi took several steps back, shrinking against the wash basin. He must have known Dorothy's hands would clench into fists when she saw him, knew her anger would bubble up again and wonder what other ju jitsu moves her muscles still had memories for.

"Can we talk?" he asked.

Dorothy felt Solomon rub against her legs. Her shoulders relaxed and her fists unclenched, though her jaw remained tight. She scooped the little cat into her arms, letting him nuzzle her hair and stepped aside for Sandi. She pushed her suitcase to the end of the bed, making only enough room for herself. She looked up at Sandi still standing in the doorway as Solomon settled onto her lap.

"I panicked," he said. "I… I assumed both you and Mary Ann would be arrested."

"And that's any better?" Dorothy snipped.

Sandi looked at his feet. "No, I suppose not. But Mary Ann is younger and was far more armed.

Logically, I thought they would see her as the culprit, and you simply defending yourself. I was wrong."

Dorothy didn't speak. She let Sandi shift uncomfortably in the door frame for several moments, continuing to scratch Solomon behind the ears.

"I find it foolish and a complete waste of time to question you. I know you are working for, or with, Robbie Hodge. How and why doesn't matter. We all seem to have the same goal, and that is where I want to focus on right now."

Solomon jumped from Dorothy's lap, discovering the food she had put in his bowl. She gasped when he launched off her knee and noticed it was swelling.

Sandi stepped forward, his hands held out before him. "May I?"

That same cautious fear rose in Dorothy's stomach again. Her trust had been violated in so many ways. But somehow, she knew that if she kept herself buried inside, never accepted an olive branch, she'd never recover. She gave a single nod, and let Sandi kneel before her, his hands poised over her knee as he worked with his *chi* energy.

"I used to do this for your father," Sandi said when he finished.

He finally looked Dorothy in the eye and did not turn away. It was uncustomary for Chinese to hold eye contact, but she felt a sincerity from him that he was desperately trying to convey, whether or not she wanted to believe it.

"Sandi, do you know what happened to my father?"

The man hung his head, his eyes focusing not on the handle of Dorothy's suitcase, but on a distant memory.

"Does it have anything to do with *Materia Prima*?" Dorothy prompted.

This time, when Sandi met her gaze, the lines around his mouth and eyes were more pronounced. "It has everything to do with—"

Solomon bounded away from his food, batting at the main door handle again just as a shadow passed beneath it. There was a knock and a whispered voice.

"Ms. Fennec?" said Tatiana.

Dorothy couldn't move. Everything she had been working towards, the reason she joined the Foxes at all, was moments away from being revealed. "Tell me," she pleaded, her heart pounding.

Sandi stepped toward the door as Solomon still pounced at the handle. "Once I do, there's no going back."

He opened the door, and Tatiana startled at seeing him, the food tray in her hand clinking as she jumped. She paused only a moment, then entered, setting the tray on the dresser as Dorothy's stomach rumbled again.

"I hope you like *solyanka*," Tatiana said, passing a bowl of soup to Dorothy. "We had it left over from the meal yesterday."

The succulent steam rose into Dorothy's face, and she suddenly didn't care what they called the dish. She took a bite, letting the sweet and sour taste rove over her tongue. She swallowed and took another bite, then another. She could feel the warmth rolling down her throat and landing in her stomach. She handed the bowl back to Tatiana and accepted a glass of sparkling water. She wanted to eat more, but as it had been almost twenty-four hours since her last meal, Dorothy needed to pace herself. There were far more pressing matters to attend to, she was reminded as Tatiana stood beside the dresser.

"I think it's only fair to tell you that venturing down this path is dangerous. You have a daughter and a family. If you wish to change your mind, I completely understand."

Sandi's mouth fell open. "What are you doing?" he whispered.

"I'm doing what my father would have done."

Tatiana paused only a moment as Sandi's Babel ear cuff translated his Mandarin to Russian. "No, something's going on. If this involved my family if they—we—are in danger, I need to know."

"Very well." Dorothy glanced at the clock, then at Solomon who was now kneading at the pillows on the bed beside her. "Come back at nine o'clock. I need to get some rest."

"I should look while—"

"No!" Both Dorothy and Tatiana cried.

"You'll wait in your room. I'm sorry, Sandi, but I can't completely trust you. Not yet," Dorothy said.

"We don't have time—"

"I'm aware we don't have time!" Dorothy shouted, and Solomon shrunk into the pillows. She took a deep breath, knowing full well she would turn into the crabby old lady of everyone's nightmares if she didn't get some sleep soon. "If Hodge wants us working together, then we're doing this my way."

"I'll make sure he doesn't leave," Tatiana said, glowering across the room at Sandi.

Sandi looked back and forth between the two women, his mouth still hanging open. When neither said anything more, he squared his shoulders, bowed, and trudged back into his room.

Dorothy let out an audible sigh. Sandi was probably dialing Robbie to complain. She didn't care. Solomon nudged her elbow, mewing softly.

"Maya usually retires to her room to read around

nine. I'll come back then." Tatiana set the bowl of *solyanka* on the tray and slipped quietly out the door.

Dorothy lugged her suitcase to the floor and kicked off her shoes. She barely had enough energy to put on a nightgown and crawl into bed. Her eyes physically hurt, and the headache she had been staving off was coming back with a vengeance. Solomon curled into the crook of her neck, resting his head across her cheek. Dorothy felt every muscle in her body relax as she drifted into sleep.

THIRTEEN

DOROTHY WOKE NOT TO THE SOUND OF HER phone alarm, which had somehow been silenced, but to Solomon licking her hair. She pushed him away, her hand coming to rest on his neck where she lovingly scratched him. She took a deep breath, taking in the smell of… that was not the smell of her fabric softener. Her memories came back to her all at once, leaving her lightheaded for a moment. She rolled over and grabbed her phone. It was 8:33 pm.

"Great," she mumbled disgruntled.

Solomon licked her hair again, and Dorothy pressed her forehead between his ears. She remembered the carefree mornings waking up to this, with Solomon's purrs lulling her out of sleep. Frank was usually awake already, and she'd open her eyes to his smiling face watching her, their cat curled between them. With

Red, Dorothy was usually the first to wake, and she would catch herself watching him sleep as Frank had with her, Solomon curled between them.

She could leave, she thought. She could leave right now. Pack everything, hop on a plane, and fly back to the States. She'd tell Destin to shove it and leave her in peace so she could return to her blissful naivety and enjoy her retirement.

But Robbie's words hung thick in the air. The Constellation Egg was more than an amulet that made cats disappear, or a flute that caused anyone who listened to dance until they dropped from exhaustion. This was something that could change the global balance of power, whatever that meant. Likely nothing good. She couldn't sit idly by and let the world fall to pieces merely because she wanted to stay home and cuddle her cat. It was very tempting, but her morals won out in the end.

Dorothy kissed the top of Solomon's head, then slid from beneath the covers to dress before Tatiana arrived. She had just finished tying her shoes when she saw Solomon head toward the door. A moment later, she heard a muffled voice, footsteps, and a quiet knock. The little cat jumped at the door handle, successfully opening the door before Dorothy could reach it. He immediately stepped out and wound himself around

Tatiana's ankles. She smiled, and scooped him into her arms, looking over her shoulder before stepping inside.

"I wanted to make sure Maksim was gone," she whispered. "I set him to guard Mr. Sandi's door while you slept."

Dorothy raised an eyebrow. Tatiana had changed from her classy funeral attire to something far more casual. She was dressed head to toe in black, with black work boots laced tight around her ankles, and her long blonde hair pulled back into a tight bun. She released Solomon, removing a bag situated on her shoulder. She withdrew a large hunting knife and promptly hung it from her waist.

"I know what you're thinking, Ms. Fennec," Tatiana said, her tone firm. "But the last time I let someone take control of my life it ended in divorce and a heartbroken daughter. We'll not even speak of the financial and emotional mess that involves me. If you intend to use my home and my family, then you're going to do things my way."

Before Dorothy could speak, Solomon's friendly trill pulled their attention away. He stared at the space beneath the bathroom door, and Dorothy wrenched it open before Sandi could finish raising his hand to knock. Once again, the little cat greeted him with ankle rubs and purrs. He may have been more trusting than she preferred, but Dorothy couldn't deny his use as an alarm system for visitors.

Sandi bowed in greeting to both Dorothy and Solomon. His expression grew sorrowful when he saw Tatiana, but he still managed a bow to her as well before asking, "Are you sure you want to do this, Fennec?"

Dorothy looked at Tatiana, who stood steadfast and silent beside the dresser, arms folded, and one black boot propped against the baseboard.

"This is your last chance, Tatiana. I won't hold it against you if you want to back out now. This is gravely risky. For both you and your family."

Tatiana let out a laugh. "I've broken up more dog fights than you can count. Do you know how many teeth a dog has? How many pounds of pressure each tooth carries? Multiplied by dozens of dogs at once? I've castrated a thousand-kilo bull with little more than a bit of numbing agent in the middle of a muddy field with the fence line over sixty meters away. My entire life is about putting myself in danger for the safety and betterment of others. If you think for one moment this prissy little rich girl will back out when things get gravely risky, you have severely underestimated me."

"Very well," Dorothy said, not bothering to hide her smile. She nodded in satisfaction to Sandi and sat on the bed. Sandi shook his head, Solomon still sitting at his feet and waiting for pets.

"But first I want to know, how is it I can understand you, Mr. Sandi?" Tatiana asked.

Before he could speak, Dorothy removed the Babel artifact.

"Fennec, don't!" she heard Sandi say, though this time, the words were clear English. No underlying Mandarin whooshed in the background melodies of his speech.

She ignored his warning, carefully clipping the artifact to a very confused Tatiana. "Can you understand me?" Dorothy asked.

Tatiana narrowed her eyes. "Of course I can."

"You only can because that little artifact is translating my English into Russian. It's also translating your Russian and Mr. Sandi's Mandarin to English for me." She removed the ear cuff, Tatiana's wide eyes following the artifact in her hand.

"Can you understand me now?" Dorothy asked. Tatiana's confused expression answered her question, and she returned the artifact to her own ear once more. "This is an artifact, taken from the city of Babel by the organization I work for."

"Organization?" Tatiana asked.

"Fennec, no," Sandi protested, appearing as if the

conversation had gone a step too far.

"After all she's been through, she has a right to know."

"It's too dangerous for her."

"I can keep your secret if that's your concern," Tatiana reassured the pair.

Dorothy held up her hand, silencing Sandi. "We travel the world collecting and neutralizing dangerous artifacts." She turned her eyes back to Sandi. "I'll say no more."

Sandi crossed his arms, clearly frustrated but pacified for the moment.

"Is that why you're here? Is... is there an artifact here in St. Petersburg?"

"I'm sure you're familiar with the Constellation Faberge egg?" Dorothy began.

Tatiana furrowed her brow and joined Dorothy on the bed. "Of course. But it's never been found."

Dorothy nodded. "Yes, there's a reason for that. Just before the Bolshevik Revolution, Nicholas II put a plan in place that, he thought, would ensure his heir's return to the throne. Do you remember when you told me Egor visited the royal family before their death and escaped with several heirlooms?"

Tatiana clasped her hand to her mouth. "No..."

"That artifact holds immense power. One that could

change the balance of control across the world."

"And Grigory was the last descendant or guardian of it," Sandi said, finally seeming to give in to the fact their party had now grown by one more.

"He willed the artifact to the organization I work for a long time ago." Dorothy paused as Solomon jumped on the bed and curled into her lap. "Your Uncle Yury changed your grandfather's will several months ago, yes?" she asked.

Tatiana nodded, her eyes widening more with each passing moment, until Dorothy worried she might actually strain them.

"Last night, we encountered another group of people trying to get the egg. The same group Yury made a deal with and the reason the will was changed."

"That's what Maya meant," Tatiana whispered. "She told me Yury didn't want people coming into the house because he was trying to protect something. She told me he only cared about the money. I didn't know that's what she meant. I couldn't have known. Yury used to be fine with the idea of the renovations and tourists. I thought she was just upset and making up stories." She buried her face in her hands in frustration. "I should have listened to her."

"Tatiana, it's vital that we find the artifact before the constellations in the sky above the Winter Palace align with the Constellation Egg," Sandi pressed.

"We need to get back to the Hermitage," said Dorothy. "We think that's where the artifact is hidden."

"Consider it done," said Tatiana. "I can make the call right now."

"What?" Sandi stepped forward, and despite his height, Tatiana leaned back unexpectedly.

"I'm a sponsor of the Hermitage," she explained.

"A sponsor?" Sandi asked, his tone rising in suspicion.

"Where do you think some of their displays came from? I donated heirlooms and paintings and all manner of things my family had collected through the years. Some of the things in the basement still need taken there. I have influence with them. I can easily call in a favor."

"Wait," said Sandi, holding up his hand. "You donated artifacts?"

"Yes, of course," said Tatiana. "Why?"

Sandi turned to Dorothy. "What if the artifact isn't in the Hermitage at all? What if it's still here?"

"In the basement?" asked Tatiana rather incensed at being ignored. "I think we would have known."

"Not if it was hidden," Sandi pressed.

Dorothy held up her hands, silencing them both. "If the artifact was indeed hidden in the basement, I find it unlikely Yury, or even Grigory, would have allowed Tatiana to donate anything to the Hermitage. Besides, the museum is where Robbie and Mary Ann believe the artifact is, and we don't know what information they have that's different from ours. Unless, of course, you'd like to weigh in on that." Dorothy gave Sandi an incredulous look.

He stepped back and shook his head. "I'm afraid I can't give any more information. Mary Ann is working on her own. But I think our search should begin here."

Dorothy let out an audible breath and felt her jaw tighten. "We can look through a few things before we head down the tunnel. Fair?" she asked, trying to keep her tone from rising in frustration. Sandi was the hardest person to read she had ever met. She wished she knew what motivations he had, what made him so defiant once he settled on an idea. Perhaps it was the computer engineer in him talking.

Sandi bowed his head. "Yes, thank you."

Tatiana slapped her thighs and rose, adjusting the knife on her belt. "I'll make sure everyone's gone to bed then. I'll be back in a moment."

She slipped out the door, barely keeping Solomon from bolting into the hall. When her footsteps had faded, Sandi rounded on Dorothy.

"You can't bring her into this."

"I would remind you that keeping secrets led to my arrest and both Solomon *and* Tatiana nearly getting killed. Forgive me if I am less than favorable toward keeping anymore."

"Be careful, Fennec. When too many people know about us, about what we do and the power we hold... I think you'll find keeping that secret far more favorable."

Dorothy lifted Solomon's carrier onto the bed, drawing the little cat's attention. He made a running leap and landed square inside, kneading the cushion and turning in a circle, clearly pleased with himself. He stood patiently still, purring and nuzzling her hands as she attached his harness.

"Is that what happened to my father?" Dorothy asked, zipping the carrier shut and hoisting it onto her shoulder.

Sandi shifted uncomfortably under her gaze.

"You said you'd tell me."

"I know. But not here, not now." He tapped the Babel artifact on his ear.

Dorothy wasn't sure if he was indicating Destin might be listening, or a more ambiguous reference to his ever-looming presence. Either way, she huffed, folding her arms across her chest, ready to unleash the sharpness of her tongue she'd been holding back.

The door opened again, and Tatiana's head poked through. "Come on," she whispered and disappeared into the hall.

The trio crept quietly down the back utility stair, pausing at each landing and straining to hear for any voices. There was the faint sound of snoring from the second floor as before, which Tatiana informed them was her mother, Vera. They continued on, emerging into the kitchen where they tiptoed through to the dining room, and into the main hall. Dorothy paused as they crept past the murals. She felt Solomon flip around in the carrier and hurried on before he could start meowing.

Sandi and Tatiana stood waiting at the elevator which Tatiana had sent down to the first floor earlier that evening. She pulled back the gate, waiting for Sandi and Dorothy to step inside. Solomon shifted again, and Dorothy instinctively shushed him as the elevator bumped and began its descent into the basement.

Tatiana bounced on her heels beside Dorothy. "I can't believe I'm doing this," she whispered.

Dorothy set a hand on her shoulder, and Tatiana stilled, locking eyes with the woman.

The elevator eased to a halt. "Are you ladies having second thoughts?" Sandi asked, stepping out.

Tatiana shook her head. "I'm coming," she said,

pulling a flashlight from her bag and marching past Sandi into the dark basement.

"I still don't like this," Sandi whispered.

"Noted," Dorothy snipped, pulling out her own flashlight, and following Tatiana through to the room with the large crates.

Much to Sandi's disappointment, most of the crates held Tatiana's furniture and possessions from her divorce. He continued to look over the art pieces that lay littered throughout the basement, taking cues from Dorothy on time-period and construction. They heard the clock in the library above chime ten o'clock, and Sandi finally accepted defeat.

They climbed through the hole Dorothy had made in the brick, trying not to disturb the crime scene tape that was still in place. Dorothy tested the grip on her cane, ensuring the blade could be unsheathed quickly, and she saw Tatiana do the same with the hunting knife in her belt.

Sandi momentarily handed his flashlight to Dorothy, digging in his fanny pack and extracting his phone. Once again, Dorothy was amazed at his packing skills. He pressed a series of buttons as they walked, the screen casting an ominous aura around the party as they went.

They trudged through the tunnel for what felt like

several miles, longer than Dorothy had remembered from their first time. The only sound was their feet on the ancient brick and Solomon's occasional chirp when he realized the tunnel echoed. They could just make out the outline of the door ahead and the reflection of more police tape when Sandi called for them to stop.

"What is it?" Tatiana asked, her hand poised above the knife.

Sandi pressed more buttons. "I need to disable the security system," he whispered. "Before we get too close to the door and activate the motion sensors."

"The security system?" Dorothy asked.

"And give us a distraction."

Dorothy leaned over his shoulder, staring at the phone screen. She watched what looked like security footage in the bottom right corner. A thin man with a sleek ponytail suddenly leapt from his desk, looking at the monitors in front of him. He pulled a radio from his belt, listening and replying back in short bursts. Then he tore from the room, sending a stack of papers on the desk flying. Sandi smiled smugly at the man's retreating back before switching to another screen. Dorothy narrowed her eyes at him.

"What did you do?" she demanded, trying to keep her voice down in the echoing space. Solomon still meowed in return, and Tatiana hushed him.

"As I said, I gave us a distraction," Sandi replied. "While you and Mary Ann were busy fighting with each other yesterday, I slipped away and hacked into the Hermitage's computer system. I can now control the entire network from my phone. The surveillance feed, the alarm system, even the keypads on the doors." He lightly ran a finger across the mesh door of Solomon's carrier, and the little cat rubbed his cheek against him. "You aren't the only one with skills in this organization, *nǚ shì*," he said.

Dorothy felt her cheeks flush as Sandi slipped the phone into his pack and headed up the tunnel. She knew Destin had selected each of the Silver Fox agents for both their location in the world and their proficiencies. But it was sometimes easy to forget she wasn't alone, that there were others she could rely on. That she was *supposed* to be able to rely on, anyway.

The sound of the creaking door to the Hermitage pulled Dorothy's attention back. She turned her flashlight and watched as Sandi and Tatiana pulled the door open, carefully looking past the police tape. She quickly joined them as they stepped past the tape and into the room beyond.

"Can you turn on the lights with that?" Tatiana whispered to Sandi.

Sandi extracted his phone again, but Dorothy was

faster. Or luckier at the very least. Her flashlight panned over the door that would have led to the basement hall of the Hermitage and over a light panel to its left. She crossed the room in careful strides and flipped them on. Sandi looked up, his hand still poised over his phone screen.

"Skills," Dorothy goaded and heard Tatiana unsuccessfully stifle a snort as they turned their attention to the contents of the room.

Dorothy had once visited the basement of the Hermitage, though it was only in the public areas. She peeked into the hall, hoping her memory might serve in figuring out their location in proximity to the above museum. The hall was lined with painted white brick, just like the surrounding room. Metal doors lined the way, each with an ominous keypad beside it. Solomon huffed and flopped in his carrier. Dorothy closed the door and set the carrier on the floor. It may have been against her better judgement, but Solomon had proven himself time and again to be her greatest asset on missions. She unzipped the top, clipping the leash to the little cat's harness before he jumped out.

Tatiana scoured a tall wooden shelf lined with dusty boxes of paperwork, and Sandi was on his hands and knees searching under desks and behind boxes looking for who knew what. Probably secret compartments of some kind, if Dorothy were honest. Solomon sniffed the air and began hunting the edges of the room. She had no idea what he was sensing, or how to impart to him what he should look for. Not that *she* knew what they were really looking for. The Constellation Egg wouldn't be hidden in plain sight in a museum with no one noticing for over a century.

Several strange figures stood scattered around the room, covered in sheets and tarps. Dorothy pulled back the covering of one, revealing a replica of David underneath. She furrowed her brow. Museums would store art pieces waiting to go on display or be transferred to another museum, but not like this. These were completely out of place. Her mind worked as Solomon tugged on the end of his leash. She dropped it, moving on to the next covered statue, this one a bust of Beethoven on a pedestal. Yes, these statues had nothing to do with each other, except that they were each made from alabaster. But why were they placed so haphazardly throughout the room?

An idea sprang to Dorothy's mind. She picked up the small David replica and flipped it over. No hidden compartments.

"Damn," she whispered to herself.

But the floor was made of simple wooden boards. Easy to hide something under. She pulled aside the pedestal, dropping to her knees and knocking on the surrounding wood.

Tatiana set aside the paperwork she had been sifting through and joined Dorothy. "What is it?" she asked.

"I don't know exactly," Dorothy said. "But these statues don't belong here, I can tell you that much." She continued to search, filling Tatiana in on her suspicions. Before she had finished, both Tatiana and Sandi were pulling back the coverings of the statues and searching for hidden compartments.

Dorothy used her cane to push herself to her feet, her left knee giving a resounding crack as she stood. She stretched then hobbled to a statue she almost hadn't noticed sitting behind the door to the tunnel. This one wasn't covered, and even from a distance, Dorothy could see it had very little dust collected on it. She pushed the door aside and gasped.

It was a cat. She knelt immediately, her hand searching over the figure for any kind of break in the smooth stone. She felt over the ears and down the back, traced each paw and the carved line of fur up its belly. Her fingers stopped at the base of the statue's neck. Her hands began to shake as she tipped the statue back, revealing a familiar symbol carved into the medallion that hung from the collar, and a Latin phrase carved there. *'S Rioghal Mo Dhream.*

"Sandi! Tatiana!" she called, not bothering to keep her voice down.

They ran to her, dodging Solomon and his dragging leash as they went. Tatiana dropped to her knees, looking at her family crest and motto engraved on the white cat.

"What do we do now?" Tatiana asked, her fingers tracing the carved collar and medallion as Dorothy's had.

"It could be trapped," Sandi offered, and Tatiana immediately let the statue fall back into place.

Dorothy opened her mouth to speak but stopped short. Solomon's ears pricked forward as he stared at the door to the tunnel.

"*Praded* died protecting the egg, and I will too!" said a young voice in the tunnel beyond.

Tatiana went pale, her hands flying to her mouth as she rushed forward and ripped down the security tape.

"I hope it doesn't come to that. We only need a little of your blood. Want not, waste not."

Dorothy stood and handed Solomon's leash to Sandi. He took it, staring at the back of the door as Dorothy unsheathed her sword again and the door to the tunnel opened.

"Maya!" Tatiana cried reaching into the darkness for her daughter.

"Uh-uh," Mary Ann warned moving the gun she pressed against the girl's side up to her neck.

Maya's pastel blue pajama's visibly shook. She bit her lip, holding back a wave of fear as she stared into her mother's eyes. Tatiana heeded the warning. She took a step back into the room, her hand coming to rest on the hunting knife at her side.

"Leave the girl alone, Mary Ann," Dorothy said, making sure the woman saw her weapon. It wasn't her first choice, but it had been effective so far. Not for the first time, she wondered if Destin had other reasons for forcing her to leave her Smith & Wesson back in Massachusetts. She only hoped her streak of good luck would continue.

"Oh, I can't do that," Mary Ann said, her voice cold and smooth, making every hair on Dorothy's body stand on end. "See, I took a detour to Grigory's estate when your friend here sent word you were at the Hermitage."

"You!" Tatiana screamed, shoving Sandi so hard he barely caught himself before landing on Solomon's tail.

"I – I was updating Robbie!"

"This wasn't his idea, love. No need to be so dramatic," Mary Ann continued. "Robbie called me, and I thought I might need a little collateral if things didn't go the way I planned tonight. And then, the most extraordinary thing happened. When I walked through the entrance hall, I found those fascinating little frescos. And do you know what one of them said?"

"'S Rioghal Mo Dhream," Sandi whispered, bending to give Solomon an apologetic pet.

"Very good, Cheng Tao. I always told Robbie you were far more valuable than he gave you credit for."

Mary Ann pulled a knife from her belt, and Tatiana fell to her knees.

"Please! No!" Tatiana pleaded.

"It's only a prick," Mary Ann reassured her. "Let's hope so any way. True innocent blood is so hard to come by these days. It's always good to know where I can find some if needed."

"No! You can't! She has hemophilia!"

Dorothy immediately resheathed her sword, holding up her hands. "Mary Ann, that's not necessary. We have Alexei's blood. You don't have to do this."

The woman gave a dramatic sigh and readjusted the gun still in her hand. "I'm afraid I'm not taking any chances."

"I'm not scared, Mama," Maya said, though her quivering chin said otherwise. "*Praded* told me everything when he made me the guardian. Everything that's happened to us—even... Papa leaving—it was all to bring me here. I'm meant to do this, Mama." Maya stood straight and held out her arm, revealing the pale, innocent skin of her wrist. "I can do this."

FOURTEEN

SOLOMON GAVE A LOW GRUMBLE, HIS HACKLES raised, and eyes dilated. Dorothy dared a glance at Sandi and watched him adjust his grip on the leash. They exchanged a suspicious glance, then turned their attention back to Mary Ann and Maya.

Tatiana's trembling form finally turned to action, her body shifting stance, ready to fight. She pressed her lips together and brandished a finger at her daughter. "Now, listen here, young lady. I don't care what your *Praded* told you, you are not a guardian or anything else. Put your arm away. Now."

Maya hung her head, lowering her arm.

Tatiana then looked at Mary Ann, still wielding her finger before her. "And you. How dare you drag my child into this. She's sixteen. Six-teen! You want the egg? Fine. But put your damn gun away and handle this like a real woman. I will not be threatened and badgered over the fate of a ridiculous piece of jewelry."

Mary Ann rolled her eyes and pointed her gun at Tatiana. "How is it humanity seems to grow more dim as time goes on? We can do this together, or I can shoot you all and take care of it myself. I've got the girl. You've got the cat. Now, which is it going to be?"

"No one is supposed to get hurt, Mary Ann. Robbie—"

"Young man, I've lived a long time and played out more situations than you can count where no one was *supposed to get hurt*. But you know what? Casualties are sometimes necessary, even if it isn't part of the plan. If it comes to it, I'll make sure you're the first to volunteer. Fair enough?"

Tatiana opened her mouth to speak, but Dorothy held her hands higher. "It won't come to that. Everyone just calm down. If we can piece together what each of us knows, then we can figure this out, and no one has to… *volunteer* for anything."

There was a pregnant pause as Dorothy took a determined step toward Mary Ann, refusing to break eye contact. "Let the girl go."

Mary Ann's gaze shifted to the cane still clenched in Dorothy's hand. She didn't quite suppress the smirk that pulled at her lips, then pushed Maya toward her mother, holstering her gun.

"There, see? We're all on the same team now. That's what you wanted, right?"

"Are you all right?" Tatiana whispered, running her hands over Maya's face and arms.

Maya nodded, swallowing hard and putting on a brave face, though her chin trembled as she faced Mary Ann. "You don't have to piece anything together," she said, bending to pick up Solomon who stood sentry between her feet.

Tatiana balked for a moment, and Dorothy wondered if her mind had jumped to the threat of claws and teeth against her daughter's delicate condition. But the cat lay calm and limp in her arms, unmoving and completely at ease. She hugged him, burying her face in his neck before releasing him.

"If I reveal the artifact, you must swear that you won't hurt anyone," Maya said, straightening the hem of her pajamas and tucking a wayward strand of hair behind her ear. "Mama, Yury, everyone in the whole world."

"Maya, you don't have to do this, dear." Dorothy reached out a gentle hand, but Maya narrowed her eyes, pulling away.

"I know you have secrets too, Ms. Fennec," she snapped, sounding impressively like her mother. "I wanted to trust you. I thought Solomon was a sign from *Praded*. But you're a liar too. You don't speak Russian, and you obviously aren't here to pay respects to my great-grandfather."

"Maya, you don't underst—"

The girl shook her finger at her mother, silencing her. "No, *you* don't understand! Hemophilia is passed through the bloodline of Queen Victoria, which makes our blood royal. Not just anyone can be a guardian. *Praded* had the disease too."

"Is this true?" Dorothy asked, turning to Tatiana. "Grigory suffered from hemophilia?"

"Yes, but I didn't think it had anything to do with… with *this*! How could I?"

"You couldn't," Maya snapped. She gave an exasperated sigh and suddenly seemed to soften. "This was all destined to happen." She turned toward her mother, her eyes unfocused and lost in memory. "I felt so alone when we came here. That's why *Praded* brought me to the museum. It… it was our special place."

Tatiana touched her daughter's cheek, her face relaxing into a comforting smile. "I know it was. You were so very special to him."

Maya took another breath, and Dorothy saw tears in her eyes. "When I learned the museum had cats, I begged him to take me to see them. He didn't want to. He was afraid I might be hurt, but he finally did. That's when it sort of... happened. The cats, they all acted strange. They'd circle around me, and they kind of... moved with me. That's when *Praded* told me everything. He told me how his grandfather passed guardianship to him when he came to the museum. Except that was when the cats were still up in the main area. They followed *Praded* from room to room until the security asked them to leave. That's why the cats were eventually moved down to the basement. They'd cause a scene anytime certain people with hemophilia came in."

This time, Maya's chin did tremble, and she let her tears finally flow. She wrapped her arms tight around herself, a single sob escaping her lips before continuing.

"*Praded* said the egg was never to be disturbed unless the fate of Russia was in danger. He said the only way to get to it might cause the guardian's death, and a new guardian has to be set up first." She turned back to Mary Ann, glistening streaks staining her cheeks. "Is Russia in danger? Because if it is, I'm ready to die for my country."

"Like hell you'll die," Tatiana seethed, spinning Maya around, her lips tight again.

Maya pushed her away. "This disease has been nothing but a curse to me! I couldn't play with my friends growing up. I can't become a veterinarian like you, like *Babushka*. It's my dream to work with animals, and I've never even been allowed more than a pet fish! You help the world in your way, Mama. This is mine."

Mary Ann chuckled, shaking her head in what Dorothy could only assume was bewildered astonishment, since it was the same reaction plastered on all their faces.

"Grigory was right to choose you," she said, still shaking her head. "I promise your family is safe, and I'll do my best with the rest. But I can't guarantee that—" She suddenly drew her gun, aiming past them all and toward the door to the hall.

Solomon dodged the attack, leaping at the handle to the door. Dorothy drew her sword, realizing Maya must have quietly unclipped his leash when she picked him up.

"Stop!" Dorothy screamed.

"Go, Solomon!" Maya cried as Tatiana shielded her.

Mary Ann took aim again as Solomon took another running leap at the handle.

"It's a round handle!" Dorothy cried, trying to make her way across the room, "He can't—"

"That little…" Mary Ann seethed, turning the gun on Maya.

In a single motion, faster than she thought she

still had in her, Dorothy lifted her sword. Before her, Tatiana finally drew her hunting knife, holding it protectively in front of her daughter.

"The doors are all locked," Sandi said as the three women faced off. "Besides, it's a cat. Let it go, Mary Ann."

Mary Ann's nostrils flared, her eyes flitting back and forth between the two blades held against her. She could take one down, but not both, and Dorothy knew Mary Ann was making that exact calculation. She lowered her gun and forced a smile, asserting herself over the situation once more.

"Shall we, then, or are you not finished telling us your sad little story?"

Maya extracted herself from her mother's grasp, kneeling beside the cat statue that had almost been forgotten.

"What are you doing?" Tatiana demanded.

"Mama, it's all right."

"No, this is not all right. We are going back to the house right this minute."

"Let her do this, Tatiana." The words fell from Dorothy's lips, surprising even herself. "She's the guardian. We have to trust she knows what she's doing."

"She's a *child*—"

"If you believe a magical egg can change the fate of Russia, then believe in your daughter."

Tatiana gaped open-mouthed, stumbling over her words in a string of indiscernible stutters. Sandi stepped between them, and Dorothy thought she saw the same security system on his phone as he dropped it into his pocket, extracting the decoy inhaler.

"I still have Alexei's blood," he said, thrusting the inhaler into Tatiana's hands. "Destin wouldn't have given this to us if it wasn't going to work."

"Do you know that for sure?" Dorothy asked, her eyes dropping to where she had seen the phone disappear. "Sandi, you're working for another... I don't know what, but you're a double agent. Don't tell me you trust Destin after all this."

"I do trust Destin. I just don't agree with how he handles the artifacts."

In the silence that hung between them, Dorothy swore she could hear a chorus of mews. Sandi gave her a single nod, his eyes rising to meet her gaze just for a moment and patted the phone in his pocket. Dorothy nodded back in understanding. He had control of the entire network, including the keypads outside all the doors. If he had successfully released the cats from the other rooms, if the cats sensed their guardian was close, then perhaps it would be enough of a distraction they could grab Maya and the statue and run.

"Get on with it!" Mary Ann tapped the side of her gun, the metal clinking ominously.

Tatiana stood behind Maya, rolling the tiny vial of blood between her hands. Several strands of her platinum blonde hair had broken free of their bun. She took a deep breath, tucking them behind her ears and lifted the vial toward the statue.

The chorus of meows from the hall grew louder. Reluctantly, Dorothy tore her eyes from Mary Ann as a shadow passed before the door to the hall. She watched as dozens of cats poured into the room. Young spry kittens, and old scrawny elders. Black and white, torties and tabbies in every pattern and coat length. They did not hesitate when they saw the humans gathered. Rather, they almost ignored everyone but Maya, creating a circle around the girl. They sat quietly in place, ears swiveling and noses twitching. Then, as one, they parted, making way for Solomon who led a large, fluffy tabby cat through the clowder.

Maya smiled as if greeting an old friend. "Hello, Kot'ka," she cooed, giving the cat a pet.

"What is going on?" Mary Ann demanded, clearly unsettled. Solomon snapped around, his ears laid flat and a sharp hiss escaping his usually gentle face. Dorothy smiled as Mary Ann took a step back.

"Kot'ka?" Tatiana breathed. "How?"

Dorothy had no answer. For all she knew, it was named after the prince's pet. Yet, the large cat was rather familiar, if she were honest. Unsettlingly familiar from the picture Destin had shown during her briefing. Then again, she had encountered plenty of black cats throughout the years that bore a striking resemblance in facial structure, ear placement, even mannerism to Solomon. However, none of them possessed Solomon's specific instincts. Instincts that had come in handy more than once during her missions. But there were probably plenty of cats throughout Russia named for Alexei's beloved friend.

Yes, that was the answer she was going with. It was certainly easier to believe than the idea Solomon had found and resurrected a zombie-cat from somewhere in the bowels of the Winter Palace. Although, she somehow wouldn't put it past the little black cat. As an honorary Silver Fox agent, he had his own special skills.

The movement was almost unnoticeable at first. As Kot'ka stepped aside, Dorothy watched as a shard of something dropped from the statue's mouth like a fang. They all stood staring, breath hitched, waiting for something more.

"I thought you said the guardian might lose their life," Dorothy faltered.

177

Maya shrugged, wrapping an arm around the tabby. "That's what *Praded* told me, and his *deda* told him."

"Perhaps it is a tale to ensure whoever accepts the role as guardian is willing to do whatever it takes to protect the artifact," Sandi mused.

Tatiana must have seen the movement as well. She dropped to her knees, not caring about the cats as she thrust the vial of Alexei Romanov's blood around the would-be fang.

"Careful there, little lady," Mary Ann warned, tapping the side of the gun in her holster.

Tatiana glared over her shoulder, trying to soak the fang in the blood. But there was no reaction, no other movement or any indication that the blood was doing anything. She lowered the vial and recapped it, her hands beginning to shake again as she cast around for any other ideas.

Dorothy was doing the same, assessing how and where they could escape to. The cats were transfixed on Maya and were not nearly the distraction she had hoped for. If someone could get Mary Ann's gun, or engage her enough to distract her, they could get the girl into the hall and to safety. She gripped the silver handle of her cane, ready to make her move.

"It's really okay," Maya reassured her mother, tucking another strand of hair behind Tatiana's ear. "It looks like just a little prick. See?"

Before Dorothy could act, Maya lifted her finger to the fang, pressing until a drop of blood appeared at the tip. It pooled around the fang, then disappeared up into the statue. A faint glow appeared around its stone eyes, and Maya smiled. She lowered her hand, and the statue's jaw dropped open, grabbing Maya's fingers and sinking a row of the same sharp fangs into her skin.

Both mother and daughter screamed. The cats gathered around them sat unnaturally still and quiet, watching the scene unfold with a hypnotized indifference. Solomon, on the other hand, meowed and hissed frantically. He pushed his way through the clowder of cats, smacking at the statue's mouth viciously, even throwing himself against the stone cat's solid form.

Dorothy's body twitched. She wanted to reach for him, to pull him to safety, but she refused to take her eyes off Mary Ann. Maya stood directly between them, and Mary Ann's hand still hovered over her gun. Her face was tight with concern, as she watched the scene unfold at her feet.

"Hold still. Just hold still, baby. Breathe," Tatiana instructed with a feigned sense of calm, pushing Solomon away before he could do any additional damage to Maya's hand.

THE SILVER FOX MYSTERIES

Maya took several deep breaths as blood dripped down her arm, soaking through her pale blue pajamas and pooling around the statue's feet. But the statue did not relent. Despite Tatiana's prying and Solomon's resumed attacks, it remained clamped tight around the girl's hand. Silent tears streamed down Tatiana's face, and Sandi finally pulled out his phone, feverishly searching the internet for what, Dorothy had no idea. It wasn't until Maya gave a last shuddering breath and sat staring at the statue did the fluffy tabby approach again.

"Get away!" Tatiana cried, trying to push Kot'ka out from under Maya's arm.

"No," Maya said, her voice barely a whisper. "No, I... I think I understand." Her voice strained against the pain but remained steady. She set her free hand on Solomon's back, and the little cat ceased his assault. "It has to know this isn't a mistake, that I intend to release the Constellation Egg. I have to be okay with this. *You* have to be okay with this."

Kot'ka mewed, licking at the blood on Maya's arm and rubbing against the girl until his fur was streaked in crimson. She scratched his ear with shaking fingers. Kot'ka broke from his guardian, walking in a tight circle around the statue, Maya's blood leaving a trail around the bright white alabaster. The teeth-like shards retracted, and Maya pulled her hand free, wrapping it in a large bandage her mother produced from her bag.

Tatiana pulled Maya into her, cradling her hand as her tears soaked the girl's shirt. Dorothy did her best to comfort the woman. She rubbed and patted her back but kept a watchful eye on both the statue and Mary Ann.

The statue shuddered, and a seam appeared, splitting the figure down the middle as bits of alabaster crumbled away. It opened, as if on a hinge, revealing a sapphire blue Faberge egg with intricate mother-of-pearl stars across every inch of its surface. It was more breathtaking than Dorothy had ever imagined.

Maya pulled away from her mother, taking the egg into her bloody hands. But the blood did not stain the artifact. Instead, it glowed brightly, the stars across its surface casting a pattern across the ceiling as every light bulb shattered above them.

When the shower of glass and metal ceased, Dorothy heard Mary Ann cock her gun. She looked up through the last remnants of falling glass and watched her aim at Maya.

"Very good. Now, hand it to me," Mary Ann demanded, holding out her free hand.

Maya stared from the glowing artifact in her hand, to the gun barrel aimed directly at her. When she didn't move, Mary Ann turned her gun toward one of the cats at her feet. She fired a shot that embedded into the stone inches from where the cat had stood. The cats hissed, some scattering, some drawing closer to Maya.

"That was a warning shot," Mary Ann said, turning her gun back to the girl. "I won't ask again."

Maya did not take her eyes off the gun pointed at her. She stood, taking a tentative step through the sea of glass. Mary Ann held out her hand again, but Maya hesitated. She looked at the artifact again, and the blood that still dripped slow and steady to the floor. Without warning she raised the egg above her head.

Sandi reacted first, diving in front of Maya as the sound of the gun shot clashed with the clatter of the egg as it smashed into a thousand pieces across the floor. Everyone's screams of pain or panic were lost in the chaos of the clowder of cats as they broke from the artifact's spell and ran in terror.

"No!" Mary Ann cried, falling to her knees and desperately picking up the shards of egg, her hands taking on tiny cuts from the shattered light bulbs.

Tatiana swept her daughter behind her in a single motion. "Dorothy, take Maya!" she commanded before kneeling beside Sandi.

Dorothy unsheathed her sword and grabbed Maya by the arm. Mary Ann knelt before the door to the tunnel, blocking their means of escape. She looked at the door out to the hall. Her fingerprints were all over everything in the room. Running back to the estate wasn't going to keep her from the authorities.

"What have you done!" Mary Ann screamed, but her laments went ignored as Tatiana pulled back Sandi's shirt to evaluate the wound in his stomach. "You stupid, *stupid* girl!" Mary Ann seized her gun again, and Dorothy felt Maya shrink behind her.

Tatiana reached for her hunting knife, but not fast enough. A blur flew across the room in a flurry of teeth and claws. Mary Ann cried out, dropping her gun as Solomon latched onto her wrist, yowling with rage and leading the charge as the other cats resumed their protection of their guardian. Kot'ka sank his teeth behind Mary Ann's knee, dropping her to the floor, where the other cats bit and slashed at every inch of her. Tatiana snatched Mary Ann's gun between the flurry of bloody paws, one hand still applying pressure to Sandi's wound. She looked at Dorothy, her eyes wide and fearful. There was no way she could get a shot off without hitting one of the cats.

"Enough!" Maya called, her voice echoing throughout the space.

The cats backed away from Mary Ann, though they still hiss and growled as she uncurled from her protective fetal position. A determined smile pulled at Maya's lips as she turned to her mother, staying the woman's hand against the gun she aimed at Mary Ann.

"We have to call an ambulance," said Maya, her voice surprisingly calm and authoritative.

At their feet, Sandi's clothes were soaked in blood, and his breathing weak. Dorothy pulled her phone from her pocket, handing it to Maya. Solomon sat on Dorothy's feet, his eyes dilated, and his ears flattened in warning as Mary Ann tried to stand.

"Easy, boy," Dorothy said. "She's not going anywhere."

Mary Ann, staring down the barrel of her own gun that Tatiana still wielded, began to smirk. She reached into her sleeve, and Dorothy glimpsed the same silvery material as before. She lifted her sword, but Solomon was faster. He took three steps forward, a deep growl emanating from his throat. He stared at Mary Ann, his green eyes boring into her, imparting some kind of message or warning. Suddenly, Mary Ann began to laugh, holding her hands up in surrender.

"All right, all right," she said.

Solomon sat back on Dorothy's feet, apparently pacified for the moment. Dorothy didn't have time to question what had just happened.

"Yes, we need an ambulance. Someone's been shot,"

THE BLOOD OF THE TSAR

Maya said as the sound of footsteps in the hall drew closer.

The man with the ponytail burst through the door with two security guards on his heels. Their mouths dropped open as they brandished their guns at the group. Dorothy dropped her sword and heard Maya drop the phone. Tatiana, on the other hand, did not relent the gun against Mary Ann until one of the guards had cuffed her. Dorothy felt a pair of cold handcuffs snap around her own wrist. She had no idea how she was getting out of this one.

FIFTEEN

THE WINTER PALACE WAS HOME TO THE RUSSIAN Emperors since the 1730s. Built to represent the might and power of Imperial Russia, it was a glorious feat of engineering and architecture, whose grandeur only grew more resplendent with each passing sovereign. Magnificent sweeping staircases, chandeliers dripping in gold and crystal, and gilded bas-reliefs boasted from every inch of the sprawling grounds.

Dorothy saw none of it. By the time the ambulance arrived for Sandi, it was too late. Tatiana and the man with the ponytail administered CPR for ten minutes straight, but there was no saving him. Dorothy held Maya under one arm and Solomon in the other until a second ambulance came for the girl. When the police and paramedics finally arrived, Tatiana did not stand aside quietly. Dorothy watched as she took charge of the situation, dictating orders and doing her best to explain the situation enough while glancing over certain details. It was a true testament to the power and influence she held within the city.

Mary Ann was arrested, still laughing as Solomon stared her down. Dorothy had an unnerving feeling that it wasn't the last time she'd see Mary Ann either. She clung tight to the little cat, refusing to let him go in all the chaos. The same officers interviewed her again, though they were less suspicious this time. Or, they feared Tatiana Denisnovna Anatakova. Dorothy wasn't sure which.

It was almost dawn when Maksim pulled up to the hospital with the limo, holding the door for Dorothy, Solomon, Tatiana, and Maya, whose hand was fully bandaged. He did not speak, and his stern face was difficult to read. Dorothy was too exhausted to care. She could have fallen into bed that very moment if she didn't have more pressing matters to attend to.

"I'll let you know when my flight is scheduled," she said to Aaron, mouthing a 'thank you' to Tatiana as the woman handed her a cup of steaming hot tea.

"Yes, ma'am. I'll make sure I've cleaned up all the trash and broken glass from the party."

"What?" Dorothy almost spilled her tea, and Solomon sat bolt upright in her lap where he had been sound asleep moments ago.

Aaron chuckled. "I'm joking. Everything's in order, ma'am. Have a safe trip."

"I will. Thank you." She lowered the phone, ready to push the End Call button and hesitated. "Aaron!" she cried out, hoping she caught him in time.

"Yes?"

She paused, catching her breath, not realizing her heart had begun to race. "I missed you."

"I missed you too, ma'am."

She heard the silence as Aaron waited for her to hang up. Hesitantly, she ended the call and sighed.

"Who's Aaron?" Maya asked from where she sat cross-legged on the floor. She had refused to go to bed, against her mother's insistence. Even though she was no longer the guardian of the Constellation Egg, she still felt it her duty to be involved. After everything they'd been through together, Tatiana finally yielded.

"He's my family," Dorothy replied, scratching Solomon's chin as he settled back to sleep on her lap. She blew across the top of her cup, looking across the brim at Tatiana. "How did Yury take the news?"

Tatiana sighed, resting her head in her hand. "I have a feeling the discussion isn't over, but let's say he's far more amicable to tourists now that he won't be seeing any compensation from Robbie or whoever for the egg."

Maya slumped, hugging her bandaged hand to her chest. "I'm sorry," she muttered. "I shouldn't have destroyed it."

"No," Dorothy said. "Don't be sorry. Never be sorry. What you did was very brave."

Maya gave a tight smile as her mother reached over and patted her arm.

"What's going to happen to Mr. Sandi?" Maya asked, looking between Tatiana and Dorothy.

"Destin said if anything happened to us while we were here, we were on our own. I… I don't even know his real name. Mary Ann said… Cheng Tao? That could be an alias for all I know. I have no way to contact his family or anything."

"Leave that to me," Tatiana reassured her. "The police will fingerprint him. I'll make sure he makes it safely home."

"Thank you," Dorothy said, finally taking a sip of her tea. The hot liquid washed down her throat, bringing with it not only warmth but comfort and a clearer mind. Solomon stretched in her lap, purring for a moment before falling back to sleep.

"He's a very special boy, isn't he?" Tatiana asked. "He found that cat who activated the statue. He tried to save Maya. I've never seen a cat act like that before."

Dorothy gently stroked his fur, feeling the kink at the

end of his tail. Something had happened between him and Mary Ann. It was like they had communicated. But that wasn't possible. Dorothy had been right there the whole time. Solomon had been a random stray, picked up in the streets of Tibet as a scrawny little kitten. There wasn't anything special about him, was there?

"Yes," Dorothy replied, a loving smile on her face as she watched the little cat sleep. "Yes, he is very special."

Tatiana wasted no time in arranging Dorothy's flight, but with the promise she and Solomon would come back and visit soon. Maya cried when they dropped her at the airport, but Dorothy was sure it was more for the little cat than anything else. She buried her face in Solomon's fur until he lifted his head and licked the tears from her cheeks.

"Stay out of trouble, *kotik*," Maya whispered, cupping Solomon's chin in her good hand. He pressed his cold nose into her ear, making her giggle.

"That's a tall order for such a little cat," Dorothy said, as Tatiana wrapped her arms around the woman, pulling her into a warm embrace.

Dorothy was taken aback. She hesitated, then returned

the gesture, squeezing Tatiana tight. The pair finally left reluctantly with Maksim bringing up the rear. Stepping inside, she checked Solomon's carrier was secure. This time, the ends of the zippers were locked together with clips Tatiana had given her. Dorothy waited outside her terminal, Solomon resting quietly beside her. She pulled out her cell phone, surprising herself when she dialed an unexpected number.

"*Halló*? Dorothy?"

"Hello, Hulda," Dorothy said quietly to her friend. "How are you?"

"I—I'm well. How are you?" Hulda's voice shook with concern.

"I'm fine. I just haven't heard from you in a while. How are the skyr-dogs catching on?"

Hulda laughed. "Fillip is trying to commercially package his skyr-dog sauce now."

Dorothy chuckled, her hand resting over the sleeping cat beside her as she passed the time catching up with Hulda.

Unlike the flight over, Solomon slept the whole way, which was fine by Dorothy as she caught up on some much-needed rest as well. For the first time since she left, she felt more at ease. She had people all around the world she could trust. Friends she could rely on, and that made all the difference to the vulnerability that had overwhelmed her for months.

By the time the plane touched down at the airport, her restlessness to step inside the walls of her antique shop was almost palpable. The taxi pulled up to the door of *Richard's Anecdotes* well after the sun had set. Solomon seemed to sense where they were. He meowed for the first time since leaving St. Petersburg and pawed at the carrier again.

"You just wait patiently this time," Dorothy scolded, though if he tried to make a break for it, she wouldn't have blamed him.

She opened the car door and heard the distinct sound of the bells above her shop door ring. Aaron and Red bolted out, leaving Dorothy hanging out of the car in shock. Red took Dorothy's hand, kissing her fingers and helping her to her feet before pulling her into a passionate embrace.

"What are you doing here?" she demanded between Red's fierce kisses.

"Aaron called me," Red said, resuming his kisses, though a bit less intensely.

"We were worried about you, ma'am," Aaron said, taking Solomon's carrier from the taxi. "You didn't sound like yourself."

"I wanted to surprise you, and Artie was free," Red whispered in her ear.

"Oh, I made lasagna!" Aaron announced with a mischievous smirk. "And I didn't drop the sauce this time."

Solomon cried louder, and Dorothy unclasped the locks before he did any further damage. The little cat jumped into Aaron's arms, rubbing against the young man's chin and grooming his stubble of hair. Red took the suitcase from the trunk and thrust cash at the driver as Dorothy fixed him with an incredulous look. He winked at her, then turned his attention to Solomon, scratching the base of his tail.

Dorothy stepped back, taking Aaron and Red each by the hand. She had almost lost this, all of this. Red, Aaron, Solomon, the shop. Even the ugly avocado-green door that led to her tiny apartment. Multiple times she thought she had lost this. Unwelcomed, tears formed in her eyes.

"Dorothy?" Red stepped toward her, and Aaron squeezed her hand more tightly.

"Oh, don't—I'm fine. You two go ahead. I'll be up in a moment."

She pulled a handkerchief from her pocket, dabbing at her eyes. Red kissed her forehead, and Aaron held the shop door for him, carrying on about garlic bread and the amount of sauce he had put in the lasagna. Dorothy watched them through the large glass window as Solomon led the way, bounding up the floral carpeted stairs two at a time.

"That's quite a scene you four make," a voice said as a figure emerged from the shadows.

Dorothy spun around as Destin approached. He removed his homburg, slicking back his hair and holding out a hand to her.

"Welcome home, Fennec," he said, and a smile like a proud father to their child spread across his face.

Dorothy did not accept his outstretched hand. She stared at him, unmoving, her heart beginning to race again.

"I suppose you're here for these," she said coolly, holding out the two black boxes that contained the Babel ear cuffs.

Destin's smile vanished. He cleared his throat and took the boxes, tucking them into the pocket of his suit coat. "Fennec, I want to apolo—"

"No." Dorothy cut him off, brandishing her finger at him in a very Tatiana-esque fashion. "I'm done with these secrets. I'm done with the lies. I don't know what you're hiding, but whatever it was, it killed Sandi."

"Sandi chose his own fate," Destin replied empathetically. "It was neither me nor Robbie that made him step in front of that bullet."

Dorothy felt the blood drain from her face. She stuck

her chin out and crossed her arms. "Sandi sacrificed himself to save an innocent child. A child who never would have been in danger if you had told me there was someone else looking for the egg."

"I'm not upset that you called Robbie," Destin said, and Dorothy felt every hair on her body stand on end. "I'm glad you did. I wouldn't have been able to help you in there. If it meant your safety, if it meant saving your life, then it was worth it."

Dorothy stared at Destin for several long moments. She had no way of knowing how much Destin knew about her interactions with Robbie, but something in his tone made her believe it was more than she liked. Perhaps he had been listening in, just not through the ear cuff. But that was a matter for another day. She wasn't about to stick her foot where it didn't belong. Not when the truth about her father's death had been within her grasp only to be snuffed out at the last moment. It was all too convenient.

"I need a break, Destin," she finally said. "We almost lost Caprice last year, and now Sandi. I'm not a young girl with my entire life ahead of me anymore. I have to start thinking about how I want to spend the rest of my days." She looked at the lights shining from the upper apartment. "And with whom."

Destin sighed rubbing the back of his head. For the

first time, Dorothy noticed how frail he looked. His dark hair was tipped with silver, and his eyes looked clouded. He pulled a flask from inside his jacket and took a drink as if it were a nervous habit.

"If that is your wish," he said, clearing his throat and returning the flask to his pocket.

"My wish is that you would tell me about my father. These secrets are dangerous—"

"These secrets are what saves hundreds, thousands of lives every day!" Destin snapped.

Dorothy took a step back. She had never seen Destin angry before.

He took several deep breaths, his hand inching toward the inside pocket of his coat again, but he stopped. "I can understand your apprehension. I do. Tell you what. Aaron's graduating soon, if I'm not mistaken. We'll reconvene then, fair? I won't stop you if you want to end this, give the artifacts in your basement back to me and never hear from me, or Red, or Artie, or anyone ever again."

It was the first time Destin had given Dorothy any control or power, but she wasn't blind to the fact he still did so through manipulation. She looked him up and down and suddenly felt uneasy. Whether it was a trick of the light or something else, his eyes had lost their cloudiness, and his hair had returned to its shiny black. What she wanted—what she needed—was time. And time was what Destin was giving her.

She nodded, holding a hesitant hand out to him. "Yes. Yes, that sounds fine."

Destin shook her hand, disappearing into the darkness as quickly as he had come. Dorothy waited until she could no longer hear his footsteps, which wasn't as long as she would have expected. A chill ran up her spine, making the hair on her body stand on end.

"Ma'am?" came Aaron's gentle voice from the door.

Dorothy hadn't even heard the little bells. She turned to see his concerned face looking back at her. She peered up at the windows to the apartment above. Sure enough, Solomon was there, looking down at her.

"Ma'am, are you okay?"

Dorothy shook off the uneasy feeling that filled her. She smiled and pinched Aaron's cheek as she approached.

"Yes, everything is fine," she said, and locked the shop door behind her.

WHAT'S IN A NAME?

There are nearly two-hundred sovereign states across the globe as I write this in 2019. Two-hundred countries and 6,500 different languages between the fifty-three million square miles of land on Earth. I don't know about you, dear reader, but for me, when the facts are put in perspective, I find it rather impossible to believe that how we name our offspring would be the same from one side of the world to the other.

When researching names for my characters, I rely heavily on census records. I calculate the character's age and birthplace, and then I find the top 25 names for that year and region and pick from there. Most of the time, I avoid last names unless I have to. You will find that Aaron's last name is finally introduced in this book, and eventually more of the characters' last names will come to light when necessary. For *Blood of the Tsar*, it was necessary.

Russian names consist of three parts:

First Name (or Given Name)
Patronymic
Last name (or Family Name)

The Patronymic name is what usually throws people unfamiliar with Russian naming conventions. It is created by taking the first name of the person's father and adding a gender-appropriate suffix to it; *-ovich* and *-evich* for men, and *-ovna* and *-evna* for women.

If Grigory Nikitovich Alexeev has a son and a daughter, here is their breakdown:

First (Given) Name: Yury (son)
Patronymic: Grigorevich
Last (Family) Name: Alexeev

First (Given) Name: Vera (daughter)
Patronymic: Grigorevna
Last (Family) Name: Alexeev

When Vera marries Denis Borisovich, she will take her husband's Last (Family) Name with the appropriate suffix.

Denis and Vera's children will follow the same pattern.

First (Given) Name: Tatiana
Patronymic: Denisovna (a combination of her father's first name and the appropriate suffix)
Last (Family) Name: Borisovna (until she marries)

Most Russians go by their First and Patronymic name in formal situations. When around friends and family, a shortened or diminutive form of the first name is used. Tatiana may become Tati or Tanya.

ABOUT THE AUTHOR

C.P. Morgan, or Cassandra Penelope Morgan, was born in a small town in Ohio. She comes from a family of both writers and English majors from both sides of her family.

The idea for the Silver Fox Mysteries was inspired by stories she heard growing up about her grandmothers. She also writes YA Fantasy under the name Cassandra Morgan.

Cassandra is a frequent guest at conventions and writing conferences in the Midwest area. She is a writing coach, a foster for orphaned kittens, and participates with The International Cat Association.

Connect with Cassandra!

WWW.AUTHORCASSANDRAMORGAN.COM
WWW.AUTHORCPMORGAN.COM
CONTACT@AUTHORCASSANDRAMORGAN.COM

FACEBOOK: **/author.cassandra.morgan**
TWITTER: **@AuthorCasMorgan**
INSTAGRAM: **@Morgan_Cassandra**

CPSIA information can be obtained
at www.ICGtesting.com
Printed in the USA
JSHW051742030922
29958JS00004B/22